## LONGARM GENTLY LOWERED RANDY ONTO THE BED...

But alarm bells were ringing deep within him. He pulled away from her. "Now just hold it right there, woman. You've been hurt fearful and what you're leading up to is bound to call for some lively buckin'. I sure don't want to hurt you none, ma'am."

Randy's square chin got even more solid, the dimple deepening, her blue-sky eyes flashing with midsummer lightning. "Look here, Longarm, I ain't about to let this here opportunity pass. My pa's off to Minneapolis, and right at the tail end of a long, dull summer, a man like you shows up! You got all your teeth, you don't smell like cows or horses, and you got a real pretty moustache. Besides, I can tell you're a gentleman. Now you get back down here beside me." She smiled then, her teeth dazzling him. "You can do that, can't you?"

Also in the **LONGARM** series
from Jove

LONGARM
LONGARM ON THE BORDER
LONGARM AND THE AVENGING ANGELS
LONGARM AND THE WENDIGO
LONGARM IN THE INDIAN NATION
LONGARM AND THE LOGGERS
LONGARM AND THE HIGHGRADERS
LONGARM AND THE NESTERS
LONGARM AND THE HATCHET MEN
LONGARM AND THE MOLLY MAGUIRES
LONGARM AND THE TEXAS RANGERS
LONGARM IN LINCOLN COUNTY
LONGARM IN THE SAND HILLS
LONGARM IN LEADVILLE
LONGARM ON THE DEVIL'S TRAIL
LONGARM AND THE MOUNTIES
LONGARM AND THE BANDIT QUEEN
LONGARM ON THE YELLOWSTONE
LONGARM IN THE FOUR CORNERS
LONGARM AT ROBBER'S ROOST
LONGARM AND THE SHEEPHERDERS
LONGARM AND THE GHOST DANCERS
LONGARM AND THE TOWN TAMER
LONGARM AND THE RAILROADERS
LONGARM ON THE OLD MISSION TRAIL
LONGARM AND THE DRAGON HUNTERS
LONGARM AND THE RURALES
LONGARM ON THE HUMBOLDT
LONGARM ON THE BIG MUDDY
LONGARM SOUTH OF THE GILA

TABOR EVANS

# LONGARM
## IN NORTHFIELD

A JOVE BOOK

# Prologue

*On a bright September morning, clad in linen dusters and trotting at a leisurely clip, Jesse James, Bob Younger, and Charlie Pitts rode into Northfield, Minnesota, to rob a bank.*

*Dismounting in Mill Square at the foot of an iron bridge that spanned Cannon River, the three outlaws strolled casually to the First National Bank's front entrance on Division Street. They surveyed Wheeler and Blackman's drugstore and the Dempier House hotel across the street from the bank. Satisfied that Younger and Chadwell had not overlooked anything on their reconnaissance the day before, the three outlaws repaired to J. G. Jeft's restaurant across the bridge and had a late breakfast of ham and eggs. An enterprising reporter later dug up the fact that each man had four eggs.*

*Shortly after one that afternoon, Jesse, Bob Younger, and Charlie Pitts rode back across the iron bridge and dismounted in front of the bank on Division Street. They were just finishing looping their reins over the tie rail when all hell broke loose. Three horsemen—Frank James and Cole and Jim Younger—clattered over the iron bridge, galloped across Mill square, then swept onto Division Street, shooting and whooping wildly as they rounded the corner. At the same time, two more horsemen—Bill Chadwell and Clell Miller—came charging down Division Street, punch-*

1

ing lead into the sky and whooping just as noisily as their confederates.

As the frightened townsmen scattered for cover, Jesse, Bob, and Charlie Pitts burst into the bank. "Throw up your hands!" they cried, as they vaulted over the counter.

Joe Heywood, the cashier, turned and ran for the vault to close it, but Charlie Pitts reached it before him. A grin on his unshaven face, Pitts ducked into the vault. Heywood tried to slam the vault door shut on Pitts, but Jesse grabbed him from behind and flung him back.

Jesse pointed to the safe that was visible inside the huge, walk-in vault. "Open it!" he barked.

"It has a time lock!" Heywood protested. "It can't be opened!"

"That's a damned lie!" Jesse snapped angrily. With one efficient, downward swipe of his sixgun, he clubbed the cashier to the floor.

"Where's the cashbox?" Bob Younger demanded of the two clerks. The men were standing against the back wall, their hands raised high above their heads.

The clerks were too frightened to reply to Younger. Jesse cocked his gun deliberately and leveled it at the nearest clerk, a tall gangling fellow with a bulging Adam's apple. Staring into the bore of Jesse's Smith & Wesson, the clerk swallowed mightily, his Adam's apple jiggling almost comically. Without uttering a sound, he pointed to the cash drawer by the first window.

Younger dashed to the drawer and pulled it open. He began sweeping the coins and bills into his satchel as Jesse hurried up beside him with his bag. At that moment an inner office door opened and a fellow in a black frock coat and brown derby rushed out. Before Younger or Jesse could stop him, he headed toward the side exit leading onto Mill Street. Emboldened by this newcomer's action, the clerk with the bulging Adam's apple tried to race out after him. Pitts brought up his gun and pumped two quick shots at the fleeing men. His first bullet caught the fellow in the

2

*frock coat. The force of the round sent the man plunging blindly through the door, while the clerk behind him crumpled onto his side and lay with his head propped against the wall. Rushing to the door, Pitts stepped over the lifeless clerk and fired two more shots at the man in the frock coat. The fellow had been heading for an alley, but he never reached it.*

*Pitts ducked back inside the bank.*

*Division Street was chaos. The five riders who had charged in to demoralize the townspeople were now coming under fire from a variety of small arms, rifles and shotguns, most of which were being hastily commandeered from two hardware stores further down the street.*

*One outlaw, Clell Miller, doing his best to stay on his horse and keep it from bolting amid the uproar, saw a townsman running down the street toward him. The fellow's eyes were shining with excitement, and he was cradling the shotgun he carried as gently as if it were a newborn infant. Miller watched him for a second and was about to decide he had better shoot the fool down when the man hauled himself up suddenly and squeezed off both barrels. The blast caught Miller in the face and knocked him off his horse. In his haste the townsman had loaded the shotgun with light birdshot, or Miller would have been killed. As it was, his face had been cut to pieces.*

*Furious, Miller swung back into his saddle and charged down the street after the man with the shotgun. Startled at Miller's reaction, the merchant turned and ran. Miller was almost on him and was about to run him down when a shot from a Winchester in an upstairs window of the hotel sent a round through his chest, knocking him off his horse a second time.*

*Cole Younger galloped over, flung himself from his horse, and knelt beside Miller. The man was lying face down. As Cole spoke to him above the increasing rattle of gunfire, Miller tried to push himself upright, then abruptly rolled over. Cole Younger found himself looking down into*

3

*the wide, uncomprehending eyes of a dead man. He did not pause to mourn. Snatching Miller's cartridge belt and two sixguns, Cole jumped onto his horse and rode back toward the bank.*

*Directly in his path blundered a tall, husky fellow. He seemed dazed. He kept calling out in Swedish for someone to explain what was going on, why there was so much shooting. He had been on his way to the bank entrance when the firing erupted; now, startled, dismayed, he was shambling straight for Cole Younger.*

*"Get out of the way!" cried Cole.*

*The big Swede stood transfixed, too confused to know which way to go. The outlaw, cursing furiously, fired at the man twice. The second slug crashed through his big skull and sent the Swede reeling out of Cole's path.*

*Inside the bank, Jesse was heading for the door when he turned, bent over the dazed cashier, rested the muzzle of his Smith & Wesson against the man's temple, and fired. The round punched through the cashier's skull, scattering his brains and shards of bone across the marble floor. Without a backward glance, Jesse straightened and hurried out of the bank. Bob Younger, carrying a satchel and a black overnight bag, broke from the bank after Jesse and mounted up. Charlie Pitts was the last one out. As soon as the three outlaws were mounted, they found themselves facing a hail of bullets.*

*Jesse ducked his head and yelled at Bill Chadwell, "Let's go, Bill! Let's get the hell out of here!"*

*Bill was more than willing to lead the way. He swung his horse and started down the street, the rest of the outlaws strung out behind him.*

*The merchant with the birdshot-filled shotgun had reloaded and was blasting away at the outlaws from a window across the street. Another townsman, A. E. Manning, was still firing his Remington repeating rifle at them, this time from behind an outside stairway. As Bill Chadwell led the outlaws down the street, Manning tracked the outlaw coolly*

4

and fired. Bill Chadwell, a bullet through his heart, toppled from his horse. Manning fired again. This time he caught Cole Younger in the shoulder. As Cole slumped forward, causing his horse to stagger drunkenly, Henry Wheeler, the rifleman who had shot Clell Miller from the hotel window, fired a blast that blew the hat off Cole Younger's head. But Cole managed to stay on his horse as the gang charged on down Division Street.

Through the merciless barrage, returning fire when they could and shooting into doors and windows, the gang rode on past the hotel. Frank James was hit in the leg. Jim Younger caught a slug in the face, and blood gouted from his mouth. Furious, Bob Younger leaped from his horse and, using it for cover, began firing at the merchant who held the Remington rifle. But the merchant drew a bead on the head of Younger's bay and fired. Younger's horse collapsed. Dodging behind a stack of boxes, Younger then came under fire from Henry Wheeler's Winchester carbine. Younger took a slug in his thigh.

The outlaws had held up when Younger went after the merchant with the rifle. Now one of them cried out, "We are beat! Let's go!"

As the outlaws yanked their mounts around, Bob Younger called after them, "Hold on! Don't leave me! I'm shot!"

Bob's brother Cole, already hit in the shoulder, wheeled back for Bob. But before he could reach down and haul his brother up behind him, another Northfield man discharged a load of buckshot at Bob. The buckshot shattered Bob's right elbow. Somehow, Cole managed to lift his brother onto his horse, and the two men clattered off across the iron bridge after the beaten, torn remnants of Jesse's gang.

# Chapter 1

Longarm leaned back in Marshal Billy Vail's morocco-leather chair and stretched his long legs out in front of him. As Vail pawed through the blizzard of paperwork that just kept blowing in from Washington, Longarm took out a fresh cheroot and glanced wearily up at the banjo clock on the oak-paneled wall behind Vail's desk. It was early, not yet eight. Longarm had been cooling his heels in Denver for too long, he realized. He was getting itchy for the saddle again. City life never had agreed with him, and he was pleased now at the thought that Billy Vail might have an assignment for him.

Vail cocked a bushy eyebrow at Longarm. The chief marshal had gone to flab from too much desk time, but he still had a hardness about him that showed now as he peered across the desk at his deputy. "Do you have to smoke that damn weed in here? I thought you were going to quit."

With a flick of his thumbnail, Longarm lit his cheroot. "Hanging around this pesthole is getting me nervous, chief. Besides, the tobacco smoke keeps the smell of horse manure at a distance. It also discourages horseflies."

"Well, it discourages me too. Why don't you take up chewing tobacco?"

"It's a filthy habit, chief. You got something for me on that desk there?"

7

"Yeah," the marshal replied wearily. "I have at that." Pulling a folder out from under a pile, he opened it and read the contents for a minute, then leaned back in his swivel chair, brushed a pink hand across his bald head, and looked at Longarm. Vail had the look of a man who was thinking of other, better days.

In his time, Vail had tracked and brought in his share of owlhoots. He had ranged over most of the West and a goodly portion of Mexico in the bargain. Those were the days before a hankering after security had tied him to this big mahogany desk, and Longarm had no doubt that Vail was, for a moment at least, reliving those earlier, better days.

"You remember that raid on the Northfield bank by Jesse James and the Youngers?" Vail asked.

"I don't remember it personal, Billy, but I heard about it. Don't tell me you know where Jesse is holing up?" The wounded Younger brothers, Longarm knew, had been cornered along with Charlie Pitts soon after the ill-fated robbery, and not long after that, Jesse and Frank had vanished near Sioux Falls. But that was four years ago. If Vail had a fresh lead on the James boys' whereabouts, Longarm would like nothing better than to have a go at bringing them in.

"Maybe, maybe not. I'm not sure *what* we got here, Longarm. All I know is the government wants someone to check out Northfield and the country around it. Seems some paper money—high-denomination federal reserve notes—is turning up in the area."

"What's the connection with the Northfield robbery?"

"This money is *from* that robbery. A valise containing these same reserve notes was taken by the gang. They weren't able to open the safe, so they took whatever they could get their hands on."

"And the government thinks it might be Jesse—or Frank—passing these notes?"

Vail shrugged. "I admit it don't seem likely. But there's

8

a chance of it. Either Jesse or Frank's still in the area—or someone who might know where they're holed up."

"When do I leave?"

"This afternoon," Vail snapped, with sudden satisfaction. "You can shake the dust of this pesthole, as you call it. There's a train leaving at four this afternoon."

Longarm stood up, pleased.

Vail handed the folder up to him. "Look this over before you leave," Vail told him. "And I don't mind admitting I'm a bit envious. Seems like a long time ago, and I suppose it is at that, but I thought I had a pretty good chance of runnin' down them two outlaws once. I was near ready to close the noose on them when they just up and vanished—like smoke." Vail smiled at Longarm, but it was a wintry, weary smile. "Maybe you'll have better luck."

"Thanks, Billy," Longarm said, taking the folder and heading for the door. "I hope so."

Longarm's luck vanished not long after he reached Northfield, two days later. He found the county sheriff was off somewhere, and no one seemed to know—or care—where he had gone. The local town marshal was no help whatever as the man did what he could to keep the Daisy Miller Saloon solvent. But at last the cashier at the First National Bank was able to recall—after much liquid prodding by Longarm—where the most recent federal reserve notes had been passed. The cashier's name was Paul Welland, and he was a big, bluff fellow with bright green eyes, red hair, and a close-clipped beard. He didn't act like a cashier and he didn't drink like a cashier; and Longarm was somewhat disturbed by the obvious reluctance of Welland to part with the information he needed.

But finally the man got up from his table and led Longarm from the saloon and back to the bank, where he pawed through some notes on his rolltop desk and came up with the name of a town twenty miles west of Northfield, Pine Tree City.

9

"Ain't much of a place," Welland told Longarm, as the lawman started from the bank. "It's on a bench over a dirty stream and an abandoned mill. Don't go looking for the pine tree—there ain't none."

Two hours later, as Longarm rode through the gently undulating farmland over roads rutted deeply from the many farm wagons, he found himself puzzling over the cashier. There was something odd about the way Longarm had had to nudge the fellow's memory—as if he hadn't wanted to remember where those last federal notes had been passed. And where the hell was the county sheriff? He had known Longarm was coming. Billy Vail had wired him, and Longarm had fully expected to find the man waiting for him when he arrived in Northfield.

Longarm pulled up.

He had begun to leave the small, prosperous farms behind him, spreads where the ranch hands were both plowing and raising stock. The land, far greener than what Longarm was accustomed to around Denver, consisted of gently rolling hills dotted with groves of trees and cut occasionally by brush-filled draws.

But to take note of the rolling countryside was not why Longarm had pulled up. On the clear air he thought he had heard the distant rattle of gunfire. But now, as he sat quietly, his hand resting lightly on the perspiring neck of the big black he had rented from the Northfield livery, he heard nothing except the wind in the cottonwoods beside the trail. With a shrug, he clapped his spurs lightly to the black's flanks, and rode on.

A bit later he came to the dirty stream Welland had described. He followed alongside its meandering banks for close to an hour, then glimpsed the benchland in the distance, and the abandoned mill just below it. But as he rode closer, he saw that it was not a mill, but a broken-down farmhouse. And there was no town on the benchland above it. He still had a ways to go, it seemed.

The bluff on the right side of the stream began to tower

10

over Longarm as he rode, until at last he was riding through a chill shadow, even though a bright, clear blue prairie sky stretched above him. But the chill was not from the shadow, he realized suddenly. As the hairs on the back of his neck rose alarmingly, he snapped his head to the right and saw someone aiming at him with a long rifle.

Automatically, Longarm swung his black toward the bluff and, keeping his head down, galloped toward it. The rifle above him fired, but the round landed in the grass a few yards behind the plunging black. A second later Longarm was out of sight of the bushwhacker, well in under the bluff, a few scraggly pines shielding him from the rim. Dismounting swiftly, Longarm snaked his Winchester from its boot and dug his way up the bluff's steep incline.

He was almost to the top when a shot came from a different angle. The round pounded into the bank just in front of Longarm's face; and a shower of loose soil momentarily blinded him. He flung himself flat into a hollow in the steep slope, blinked away the dirt, and brought up his rifle. But he could find no target. He didn't like his situation. There were now two men anxious to cut him down, perhaps even more. He felt like a bear storming into a hornet's nest. Only he didn't have a bear's thick hide. Keeping his body still, he looked around him, waited a moment, then continued to pull his way up to the rim of the bluff.

Poking his head at last through a thick patch of bunch grass, he saw, waiting for him, not two, but six men. They hadn't glimpsed him yet peering through the grass, but it wouldn't take long. The two jaspers who had already fired at him were crouched at the bluff's edge, peering over alertly. Behind these two, four riders sat their horses, waiting.

And in their midst sat a tall, broad-shouldered, hatless girl with long, wheat-colored hair, blue eyes, and a bosom that swelled opulently beneath the black woolen man's shirt she wore. Longarm could not see much of her face, since

11

the entire lower portion of it was wrapped brutally with a black bandanna. From the look in her eyes, Longarm could tell that the woman was almost beside herself with fury.

He pulled himself cautiously through the thick, waist-high grass, willing to measure his progress by inches. When he was fully flat in the grass, he gently pulled his rifle ahead of him and rested it on the ground, then withdrew his double-action Colt Model T .44-40 from its waxed, heat-hardened, cross-draw rig. He usually kept only five rounds in the six chambers, allowing the firing pin to ride safely on an empty chamber. But safety was not his concern now. He rapidly slipped a round into the sixth chamber, placed the big Colt down beside the rifle within easy reach, and picked up the rifle. He had a third weapon on his person, a double-barreled .44 derringer. It was tucked into the left breast pocket of his vest, and doubled as a watch fob. But he kept this deadly surprise for close-in fighting. At the moment he was hoping he could keep these jaspers well away from him.

The four riders were a good thirty yards back. They were alert but relaxed, and none of them had their weapons out. The fellow who had fired upon him first was to Longarm's right and was the closest. He was still peering nervously off the bluff, his rifle at the ready. The other one was on Longarm's left, partially obscured by a large boulder. Longarm chose the fellow who had started all this ruckus in the first place, lifted his rifle, sighted swiftly, and fired. The man was still looking down over the rim of the bluff as he toppled forward out of sight.

Levering swiftly, Longarm swung the rifle around to the other man, who had sprung to his feet at the shot and was now peering at the spot where his companion had been crouched a moment before. He made an excellent target. Longarm fired and caught the man in the forehead, just under the hat brim. His head snapped violently back, pulling his body with it, a fine red spray salting the grass behind

12

him. Once he struck the ground, he did not move again.

By this time the four riders, sixguns out and blazing, were galloping toward Longarm's prone figure. As the rounds snicked through the grass or thudded into the ground in front of him, Longarm dropped his rifle and snatched up his sixgun. His first shot caught the lead rider in the chest and he peeled back off his horse; his second shot caught the second rider in the thigh. The man cried out and swung his horse around. The two other riders broke wide, one to the left, the other to the right, and took out their rifles.

They had clear shots at Longarm now and were anxious to stay out of range of his sixgun. Longarm holstered his Colt, snatched up his rifle, and began to crawl back toward the rim of the bluff behind him. But the hail of bullets from the two riflemen became so intense that Longarm thought it prudent to hold up and dig himself into the ground. When the crown of his Stetson caught a slug, he hastily removed his hat and crushed it down beside him, cursing.

And then he saw the blonde girl riding at a furious pace toward the rifleman on Longarm's left. The man was so busy levering and firing that he did not notice the onrushing blonde fury until the last moment. To Longarm's astonishment, the girl's horse bowled into the rifleman's as she flung herself from her saddle, carrying the rifleman with her to the ground. This action so distracted the other rider that Longarm was able to snatch up his rifle, move to a crouch, and fire at the man. The round came close enough to warn the still-mounted rifleman that Longarm was firing at him. The man turned his attention back to Longarm and raised his rifle. Longarm took his time and squeezed off a shot that caught the rifleman in his right forearm, flinging it up so swiftly that it caused the rifle butt to slam into the man's jaw. The rider remained on his horse, but was unable to hold onto the rifle.

With a cry to the others, he turned his horse and galloped away. The rider with the thigh wound had been trying to

13

haul the first rider onto his horse all this while. Now, however, he gave up on his severely wounded comrade and galloped toward the rifleman who was still on the ground, wrestling with the blonde.

Longarm stood up, tracked the wounded rider carefully, and fired. His round caught the rider somewhere in the back, slamming him brutally forward. Longarm saw him grab the saddle horn, then kick his horse around. In a moment he was galloping drunkenly after the other rider. At once Longarm raced across the flat toward the two struggling figures on the ground.

As he approached, the rifleman—who was now on top of the woman, punching her in the face with measured fury—saw Longarm's running figure, snatched at the reins of his horse, mounted up, and galloped off after the other two.

Planting his crushed hat down crookedly onto his head, Longarm pulled up a moment later and looked down with astonishment at the unconscious woman lying sprawled on her back before him on the grass. Her shirt had been torn brutally, revealing one breast fully, another partially. Her face was turned to one side, and it was already discoloring from the beating she had taken. But it was not this that astonished him; it was the fact that the woman still had both wrists securely bound.

She had ridden across the flat and flung herself on that rifleman; then she had grappled and struggled with the man on the ground. Longarm had seen her giving almost as good as she got, for a while at least. And yet, all that time, the woman had had both hands tied together!

He knelt by her side, took out his pocket knife, and sliced through the bonds. Then he pocketed the knife and rubbed her wrists and hands in order to get the circulation going in them again. He heard her gasp slightly, took her jaw gently in his hand, and turned her head. She opened dazed eyes and glanced up at him. He found himself looking down into a face that contained a full, sensuous mouth with

14

cherry-red lips, a strong, square chin containing a tiny dimple, and eyes as blue as the sky that now stretched above them both. She tried to smile, but it was too painful.

"Thank you, mister," she said. "Whoever you are, you got me free of them devils, didn't you?"

"I'd say it was both us did it, ma'am. My name is Custis. Custis Long. My friends call me Longarm."

She took his hand. "I want to be your friend, too, Longarm. My name is Randy Swenson."

"You took quite a beating," he said.

"My face hurts and it isn't so easy for me to talk." But then she smiled, revealing milk-white teeth. "My, your hat is on real crooked, ain't it?"

"I guess it is at that, Randy."

She glanced down at herself and saw her exposed breasts. She gasped, her face suddenly scarlet. Hastily she drew the remnants of her cotton shirt up over her breasts, then attempted to sit up. With a startled gasp she clutched at her right side.

"What's the matter?"

"I think that devil cracked one of my ribs."

"Lie back down," Longarm commanded. "You live near here?"

She did as he had instructed, her face twisted in pain, then spoke softly to him, all merriment gone from her eyes: "That farmhouse—below the bluff."

He nodded. It was not going to be easy getting her down there. He would have to carry her, and each step would be torture for her. She wore dark woolen men's britches and he saw no sign of a corset or of any petticoats under the shirt.

"I'll just have to rip up that shirt," he told her, "and use it to wrap around your ribs while I carry you down there. Will that be all right, Randy?"

Her face was still flushed. "If you can stand to look at me, Longarm," she said, her voice curiously light. He caught something devilish dancing in her eyes.

15

"All right, then," he said.

She watched him silently and helped whenever she could as he pulled her shirt off and then ripped it carefully into strips. Sweat stood out on her forehead from the pain as she sat up and let him bind her tightly about the ribcage. Longarm was perspiring too, only it was not because of pain. Every time his big hands touched her warm, silken skin or brushed one of her nipples as he snugged the dark strips of cloth securely up under her bosom, he felt a tingle of excitement. It annoyed him slightly that he should be so susceptible to this woman's nearness. After all, this was no time for that sort of thing; the poor woman was injured. Nevertheless, he could tell that she too felt the same excitement.

"Ready now?"

She nodded. "It feels a lot better now," she said.

"What's the best way down to your house?"

"You'll have to go back that way," she said, indicating the direction with a toss of her golden head. "I'll direct you."

He carefully reached in under her body and caught her about the buttocks and under her knees, then stood up with her in his arms. She snugged her head in under his chin and wrapped both arms tightly about him. She was surprisingly light.

"Comfortable?" he asked her, bemused at the lightheadedness he felt.

"Mmm," she said softly, holding him still closer. "Very."

He started off in the direction she had indicated, his senses reeling dangerously.

16

# Chapter 2

His senses were still reeling—as much from the long walk under the hot sun as from Randy's provocative nearness—when they reached the ramshackle farmhouse alongside the stream. He had to be careful mounting the back porch steps. A few were so flimsy he was afraid his foot would crash through. One step was completely gone. The kitchen door hung on a single worn leather hinge. The smell of wood-smoke and rotting timbers hung heavy in the air as he entered the kitchen.

"My bed's in the next room, Longarm," Randy said, her mouth close to Longarm's ear.

Amid all this dilapidation, Randy's bedroom was a pleasant, almost radiant, oasis. Sheer lavender curtains hung on her two windows, the wall was recently whitewashed, and on it she had carefully hung two lithogaphed landscapes. Between the two windows sat a fine oak dresser with its large oval mirror. Spread neatly atop the dresser were Randy's amber-colored celluloid comb-and-mirror set, unguents, a music box with a dancing sprite on its lid, powder boxes, and rosewater.

But it was the bed that dominated the room. It was a canopied four-poster, set luxuriantly high off the spotless floor. The canopy was of the same shade of lavender as the curtains, as was the bedspread. The pillows were full and obviously packed with feathers.

17

After Longarm gently lowered Randy onto the bed, he found himself unable to straighten. Randy refused to untwine her arms from around his neck. Instead, she increased her pressure and pulled Longarm down beside her on the bed. As she moved aside to give him room beside her, she fastened her lips to his, and Longarm found his senses reeling even more dangerously than before.

But alarm bells were ringing also deep within him. Randy had been severely hurt. She had one, possibly two, broken ribs. In addition, there was no telling what other internal injuries she might have suffered as a result of that fearsome beating she had taken.

Longarm pulled away from her, aware that his hat had slipped from his head and was rolling crookedly on its brim along the floor behind him. "Now just hold it right there, woman," he told Randy. 'You're about to wake the fires of a devil passion in me, sure enough. And once I start to burn, it'll take more'n a summer shower to put me out. Now, you've been hurt fearful and what you're leading up to is bound to call for some lively buckin'. I sure don't want to hurt you none, so just back off, ma'am."

Randy's square chin got even more solid, the dimple in the middle of it deepening, her blue-sky eyes flashing with midsummer lightning. "Now look here, Longarm. I ain't about to let this here opportunity pass. My pa's off to Minneapolis, and right at the tail end of a long, dull summer, a man like you shows up! You got all your teeth, you got shoulders as wide as a barn door, you don't smell like cow manure or horse manure, and you got a real pretty moustache. Besides all that, I can tell you're a gentleman. Now you get back down here beside me. You won't hurt me none. I won't let you. Just be careful is all. Real careful." She smiled then, her teeth dazzling him. "You can do that, can't you?"

"But Randy, you're hurt. Hurt bad."

"I'll be hurt a damn sight worse if you don't stop all this fool palavering and get back down here where you belong."

18

Longarm smiled, shrugged, and began to unbutton his shirt. At once Randy leaned over, gasping slightly from the pain in her cracked ribs, and began tugging open Longarm's fly. He did what he could to help her, aware as always that it was a lot more dangerous to turn a woman down when she wanted to play than it was to force a woman who didn't.

In a gratifyingly short time, he had no further impediments between himself and Randy's long, silken-smooth body—except, of course, for the strips of Randy's shirt that were still bound tightly about her ribs. In accordance with her warning not to hurt her—and his own desire not to do so—he concentrated at first on warming her up, first with kisses, then with long, affectionate attention to her breasts, his tongue flicking at her erect nipples while his light, caressing hand explored her completely—but always gently.

Only when at last she began to moan aloud and had grabbed a fistful of his hair, threatening to scalp him without the aid of a knife, did he carefully spread her out before him, ease himself up onto her, and then, with exceedingly great care, enter her.

Randy gasped. "My God, Longarm," she told him. 'You know how to drive a woman wild. It ain't hurt none at all yet."

He smiled down at her. "Now just lie quiet, Randy, and let me see what I can do."

She closed her eyes and nodded.

He was mildly disappointed at the ease with which he penetrated her. So moist had she become as a result of the extended attention he had given her beforehand that at first he could barely feel the walls of her vagina closing about his erection. But now she had tightened on him like a powerful fist, and he felt himself swell magnificently. He began probing her warm depths, almost fearfully at first, until at last he could be gentle no longer. He thrust deeply, and felt her gasp in pleasure. She reached up to pull him to her, but he would not let her. He knew it would hurt her ribs. With each thrust he plunged still deeper, his fear of

19

hurting her swept away as he felt her pelvis rocking up slightly to catch each thrust expertly, deliciously.

"Longarm!" she called softly to him, her head flung back, her eyes still closed tightly. "You're in so deep, I can taste you. I swear it!"

"Shh . . ." he told her, increasing the rhythm of his thrusts. "Just lie still and enjoy it."

She did as she was told. By now Longarm was mounting inexorably to his climax. He made a valiant effort to hold back. He did not want to hurt her; but he found himself throwing aside all restraint and swept past the point of no return. He heard her gasps, then her sharp, inarticulate cries. At one point he thought she was screaming. He did not know whether she was telling him to stop or go on. It didn't matter. He was no longer the gentle, concerned gentleman. Thrashing her head back and forth, Randy, climaxing, uttered a long, low moan that rose to a high, keening scream— just as Longarm reached his own shattering climax.

Somewhat hastily, he pulled himself free and came quickly to rest beside her on the bed. "Are you all right?" he asked her, his voice filled with genuine concern.

She opened her blue eyes. They were smoky with passion still unquenched. But she smiled. "I'm fine. Just fine. That was worth waiting all summer for. Now get back over here. That was only the beginning. We've got the rest of this day and then there's tonight."

"But your ribs!"

"You know what?" She smiled impishly as she reached down with one hand to fondle him. "I think they're already beginning to knit together. If they get any worse, you can always bandage me up again, can't you?"

He smiled back at her and nodded. Already her gentle ministrations were bringing him back to life once again. He moved closer to her and began to nibble on her earlobe, while his right hand reciprocated her own devilish skills.

Hell, maybe she was right. Maybe this would help those ribs of hers to heal. One thing was for certain, it was cheer-

20

ing her up something fierce—and it was doing him a hell of a lot of good, as well.

The next morning, a tight corset serving as a brace for her cracked ribs, a cheerful Randy was standing at the stove, preparing Longarm's breakfast. She was barefoot, and over the corset she wore an apron and a long skirt. And that was all. There was nothing under the apron's straps, not even a chemise, and nothing but her long, bare, silken legs under the skirt. Watching her at the stove while he sat at the deal table, a steaming cup of coffee in his hand, Longarm marveled at the woman's beauty and stamina. Less than an hour before, awakening him with a kiss, she had prevailed upon him once again and had somehow managed to extract from his depleted body the last full measure a kind Providence had left within him.

He was pleasantly, lightheadedly drained, and he was sure the first morning breeze that found its way into this tumbledown shack would waft him away like some insubstantial dandelion seed. He needed this breakfast Randy was fixing to give him some weight, some solidity. It might also banish his giddiness and get him back to the business at hand. Satisfying the needs of an extraordinarily healthy Norse maiden who had been forced to wait too long between times was not the only reason he was in this country, no matter what she might think.

Leaning over him maddeningly, Randy delivered the full platter of eggs, potatoes, bacon, and the two thick slices of bread she had toasted on the top of the stove for him. The bread was covered generously with raspberry jam. After pouring him more coffee, Randy sat down across from him, her magnificent breasts almost completely exposed, to watch him eat. She hummed softly, contentedly, to herself. If she were a cat, she would have been purring.

Resolutely determined to eat his breakfast without being unduly distracted by her all-too-obvious charms, Longarm decided the best thing would be to start questioning her

21

about those men who had bushwhacked him the day before. More than once during the night he had made just such an attempt, each time with pathetic results. All he had been able to get from her was that she was living here alone while her father—whom she playfully referred to as the Last Great Western Bandit—was away on some business he had in Minneapolis, a full day's ride from there. But about the bushwhackers she hadn't told him a thing. This time, however, he was determined not to let her lips close his.

"You said you knew those men who bushwhacked me, Randy. I need to know who they are—and why they were after me."

She stopped humming and frowned across the table at him. "I know who they are, all right. But I have no idea why they were after you."

"You were their prisoner. They had that bandanna tied around your mouth and you were bound by the wrists. Why?"

"I rode up when they were getting in position to ambush you. I wanted to know what in hell they were doing on my land all loaded for bear, guns out and cocked. They didn't bother to tell me. All they did was tie my hands and wait for you. They wrapped that bandanna around my mouth to keep me from shouting out a warning. I told them I would, like a damn fool."

"You are a very brave girl. You likely saved my life. I owe you."

"Longarm," she said, leaning closer, "after last night and this morning, I owe you."

Still determined not to get sidetracked, Longarm plunged on. "I want the names of the men in that gang, Randy."

"Sure."

Randy got up from the table, poured herself a cup of coffee, then sat down again across from Longarm."You mean *what's left* of that gang, don't you?"

"I guess I do, at that."

22

"That son of a bitch who was beating on me is Frank Tarnell. The other two he galloped after are Brad Tarnell, Frank's brother, and Amos Lavery."

"And the others?"

"That fellow Brad was trying to haul up onto his horse, the one you caught in the chest, is Tip Wilcox. Those other two, the ones you picked off along the edge of the bluff, were Red Lavery and his brother, Tim. Guess you took care of those two for good."

"Who are they? Why were they trying to bushwhack me?"

"I didn't have time to ask, and they didn't seem to think it mattered if I knew or not."

"Are they ranchers in the area? Do they work for anyone? What's their line of work when they aren't bushwhacking lawmen?"

"You interrupted them while they were doing it. They drifted into Northfield two years ago and have been doing odd jobs like this last one ever since. They usually have better luck then they had with you. I figure this is the first time they ever messed up a bushwhack, judging from the number of dead bodies that've been turning up since they arrived."

"You think someone hired them to bushwhack me, is that it?"

"Well, now, Longarm, they don't usually *give* their services away."

"Any idea who they might be working for now?"

"No, I don't, Longarm."

"Where do they usually hole up—when it's time to lick their wounds, I mean."

"I heard tell it was in the badlands west of here, on the other side of Pine Tree City."

Longarm nodded. "What can you tell me about Paul Welland?"

"He works at the bank."

"That's right. He's a cashier. And he was the only one

23

who knew I was heading in this direction."

"You think he hired the Tarnell gang to bushwhack you?"

"Yes. But what I would like to know is why."

"Maybe you better ask him."

"I will, Randy, I will. But first I've got an unpleasant bit of business out there that has to be tended to, I'm afraid."

"I don't envy you."

"You got a shovel I can use?"

"There's a spade in the barn. I'll show you. But with these torn-up ribs, I'm not going to be much help."

"I wasn't going to ask you."

"Want another cup of coffee before you go out there?"

"The sooner I get to it, the less I'll have to contend with when I do. When that sun gets high, I'll find myself fighting off the buzzards and the stench."

At that moment the kitchen door swung open and a hulking figure stood in the doorway. It was Tip Wilcox, the gang member Longarm had shot in the chest. Despite the fact that he had the pallor of a dead man, there was a big Colt in his right hand and he was obviously still strong enough to use it.

"Tip!" Randy gasped, jumping to her feet.

"Just stay put, Randy," Wilcox told her in a rasping, hollow croak. He waggled the pistol at her and she quickly slumped back down.

Longarm realized Wilcox must have crawled all the way from the bluff. He was hatless. His bloodied chest was matted with dried grass and dirt, his Levi's heavy and stiff with dried blood. A stench hung about the man, and Longarm realized Wilcox must have fouled himself during the night. His eyes, tight with pain, peered at Longarm out of a face the color and texture of a dirty bedsheet.

"You're a dead man, Wilcox," said Longarm, getting to his feet. "Put down that gun."

"After I've finished what we started, lawman."

Longarm turned to look down at Randy. "What time is it, Randy?"

"Time?" She was astounded at Longarm's question.

24

"Didn't you say the sheriff was due here by seven?"

"Oh . . . yes, I did," she said, without too much conviction.

Wilcox's face twisted into a parody of a smile as he pushed himself further into the kitchen. Longarm could see, now, that his bullet could not have missed the man's heart by much. It was obvious from the outlaw's labored breathing that the slug must have lodged in his lung. "That's just a bluff, lawman. There's nothing could get that lazy fool sheriff out here." Wilcox began to cough raggedly, painfully. "Besides, he ain't no friend of yours."

"Just let me check my watch," Longarm told him.

Somewhat befuddled by Longarm's seeming idiocy in arguing the point, Wilcox did nothing as Longarm lifted his pocket watch from his left vest pocket. Gazing with great intentness at the face of the watch, Longarm shook his head as he rested his right hand over his right vest pocket.

"I can't understand it," Longarm said unhappily as he turned his attention back to Wilcox. "He said he'd be here by now."

"I told you," Wilcox rasped, raising his revolver so that Longarm had no difficulty peering into its bore. "That poor excuse for a sheriff ain't gonna save your bacon none this time, lawman."

"Guess you did at that," Longarm said. "There's just one thing, Wilcox. About Randy here. I want you to leave her alone. She's suffered enough already."

Wilcox looked glassily over at Randy. "No," he said thickly. "I'm going to kill her too. She's the bitch helped you . . ." He coughed again. A thin trickle of blood began to run down from one corner of his mouth.

The moment Wilcox turned to look at Randy, Longarm drew his double-barreled .44 derringer and leveled it at Wilcox. "I would drop that pistol, Wilcox," Longarm said quietly. "This derringer is small, but it packs a wallop at this range."

Stunned, Wilcox looked with slow, exasperated fury at

25

the small gun in Longarm's hand. Against all good sense, he steadied his own sixgun and leveled it on Longarm's chest.

Longarm fired—both barrels.

Two fresh holes appeared in Wilcox's chest. He rocked back, sudden astonishment registering on his face. As his knees collapsed under him, he squeezed the trigger of his Colt. Longarm flung himself to one side as the big gun thundered in the small room. Behind him, the bullet whanged loudly into the kitchen stove and ricocheted up into the ceiling. Wilcox was sitting down by this time, his back against the wall, the big sixgun still in his hand. He coughed and tried to say something, then slowly tipped over like a broken toy, the Colt slipping from his grasp.

Longarm got to his feet and saw Randy pulling herself up from behind the table, where she had flung herself when the shooting began. "You all right, Randy?" he asked.

"I don't feel so good," she said. "I guess my ribs are acting up some. That was a dead man walked in here, Longarm." She shook her head. "Hard to understand how he could have made it this far."

"Pure, cussed meanness, I suspicion," said Longarm. "Anyway, this is one jasper I won't have to climb that bluff to bury." He reached down and grabbed the dead man by the back of his vest and began to drag him toward the door. "You said that spade is in the barn, didn't you?"

"Yes," Randy said, still shaken. "I think I'll go into the bedroom and lie down for a spell."

"You do that, Randy," Longarm replied, as he pushed open the door. "I'll be back when I'm finished."

As the kitchen door banged crookedly shut behind him, Longarm took a deep breath. Despite the corpse he was dragging, the fresh brightness of the morning reminded him how good it felt to be still alive. That pesky little derringer might sit a bit heavily in his vest pocket at times, but he sure as hell had never complained—and never would.

26

# Chapter 3

It was a little before ten that morning, Longarm reckoned, before his grisly task was completed.

Longarm had found Red Lavery sprawled at the foot of the bluff, a bullet hole through his neck, a full complement of vultures having pulled up chairs for the feast. The vultures had been a bit testy at the prospect of losing their morning meal; but Longarm had waded in among the humpbacked diners, flailing his spade about with mean precision. So sluggish had their gluttony made them that even at such an early hour they had difficulty lifting into the quiet air.

Longarm had buried Lavery on the spot, planting his buddy, Tip Wilcox, right alongside. He did not bother with markers. Lavery's brother had been where Longarm had dropped him, close by the edge of the bluff, the back of his head gone, his brains already leached into the soil under him.

Now, leaning wearily on the spade's handle, Longarm lit up a cheroot, grateful for the smoke's ability to banish from his nostrils the stench of death, and let his eyes idly follow the line of the bluff. At once he was alert. More vultures were wheeling about in the sky above a spot at least a quarter-mile farther back along the bluff. So busy had he been planting corpses, he had looked up hardly at all, or he would have noticed the circling buzzards earlier.

27

Longarm was not anxious to investigate. More than likely, it was the body of that jasper he had hit in the thigh. According to Randy, that would make him Brad Tarnell. Still, it was unlikely his brother Frank would abandon him, no matter what his condition. So perhaps it wasn't Brad Tarnell. Someone else, then.

That was when Longarm remembered what had alerted him the day before—the sound of gunfire in the distance. With a sigh, Longarm rested the handle of the spade on his shoulder and started for the feasting buzzards. A brisk walk took him to the site. Longarm thought he recognized a few of the buzzards he had driven from Tip Wilcox's body. They glanced sidelong at him, their insane eyes glaring at him, then lifted obscenely into the air, their great black sails catching the warming air currents and lifting them into the cloudless sky.

Moving closer to the remains, Longarm saw at once that the body was not that of Brad Tarnell. Instead, sprawled faceup on the ground before him was the body of Paul Welland, the cashier at Northfield's First National Bank. There was not much left of his face, but his dress and general appearance were all Longarm needed to make the identification. With the toe of his boot, Longarm turned Welland over and noted the large, ragged holes where the two rounds that had entered his chest from the front had exited.

Unhappy at the task before him, Longarm knelt by the body and searched the man's pockets. What he found were an empty wallet that appeared to have been stretched to capacity not long before, some IOUs, and, folded neatly in a compartment of the denuded wallet, a scrap of paper.

Longarm stood up and unfolded it carefully. On it was neatly transcribed a list of the missing treasury notes. What caused Longarm's eyebrows to rise, however, was the length of the list. It was considerably longer and more detailed, in terms of denominations, than the one Vail had given Longarm in Denver. At the top of the list Longarm

28

saw the initials "C.F.," and beneath that, in a cryptic sprawl, "The Best," in what Longarm judged to be Welland's handwriting.

Pocketing the list, Longarm set about planting still another corpse—if only to rob those damned buzzards still sailing impatiently above him. As the dirt flew over his shoulder, he comforted himself with the fact that he would soon be away from this killing ground, on his way to Pine Tree City—and perhaps some answers to go with all the questions this last torn body had raised.

Toward evening of that same day, Longarm found the abandoned mill on the bench overlooking the dirty stream—and beyond it, Pine Tree City.

As the dead cashier had told him, it was not much of a place, nor was there any trace of a pine tree. The town was a collection of weathered, unpainted shacks clustered close in under a ragged bluff that lifted wearily up from the bench. Riding into the town, Longarm passed what had probably once been a fairly prosperous general store, and beyond that a hotel that boasted a full three stories. But these were the only signs of Pine Tree City's prosperous past.

What remained in all their former glory, however, were the four saloons, one on each corner of the town's single intersection. The biggest one, and obviously the saloon that boasted the meanest clientele, styled itself the Cowboy's Palace. The others were less flamboyantly named, and did not have as large a porch. From behind the batwings of the Cowboy's Palace, a few bar girls and prostitutes peeked out at Longarm, their painted lips in sharp contrast to their flat, sunless faces. Perched on the porches of each saloon were the saloons' patrons, the noxious weeds that sprouted so readily from such bitter soil. A few of the men sat on the porch flooring, their backs to the posts, while others lazed back on the tops of barrels or straight backed chairs. All of the men Longarm glimpsed were hardcases; the only

29

things clean and bright about them were the guns strapped to their thighs.

As Longarm rode past the corner on his way to a dilapidated barn that advertised itself as Hank's Livery, he felt their cold, dead eyes resting on him. Despite a long, hot ride under a sun that had thoroughly baked his neck and shoulders, he felt a chill run up his spine. The chill of death. These men were the human vultures that not only picked corpses clean, but created them as well.

A one-legged ancient, his face hidden almost completely behind a disordered gray beard, swung out of the livery's dark interior on a single battered crutch. He watched with bright, squinting eyes as Longarm dismounted and led his black past him into the welcome coolness of the stable. The smell of horse piss and manure was heavy in the place. It was obvious that Hank was not able to keep his stable as clean as a whistle while hobbling about on his crutch. It was also obvious to Longarm, as the fellow leaned back on his crutch and watched him select a stall that was not entirely filled with horse manure, that the old man did not much care.

"You Hank?" Longarm asked when he had finished unsaddling the black, brought him water, then filled his feedbag with fresh oats.

"That's right," the oldtimer said, expectorating a black arrow of tobacco to the floor a few feet to his right. "That'll be fifty cents."

"What for?"

"The use of the stable and the oats, mister. Ain't you never heard of a livery stable before?"

"Seems like I'm doing most of the work."

"Seems like you did it right passably too. No sense in my getting in your way with this here crutch when you was doing such a fine job. You take good care of your horseflesh, mister. I noticed that right off. It was a pleasure watching you."

Longarm gave the graybeard fifty cents. "I'd like some information, Hank."

30

"That'll come expensive, mister." The old man held out his hand.

Longarm passed him another half-dollar. "I'm looking for Frank and Brad Tarnell. I got good reason to believe Brad's been wounded. You might have heard."

"I ain't heard nothing. But that don't mean a thing. I never get the good news until its ridden on past me."

"Is there a doctor in this town?"

"Don't seem likely, does it?"

"I'm asking."

"Sure. We got a doc, and he didn't get his medicine bag from no mail-order catalog, neither. His name's Gurney."

"Where can I find him?"

"The Cowboy's Palace. He's either holding up the bar or sleeping it off on a poker table in back. If you got a toothache, mister, I'm warning you. His hand ain't as steady as it used to be."

"Thanks," Longarm said, moving past Hank and out into the dusty street, heading for the Cowboy's Palace. It wasn't himself he was thinking might be needing the services of this sawbones.

Doc Gurney was not holding up the bar at the Cowboy's Palace, nor was he sleeping it off on a poker table. As Longarm entered the saloon, he caught sight of the old sawbones sleeping in a chair at the rear of the saloon, his tattered black medicine bag on the table in front of him. The man's hat was off and his frail head was resting back against the wall as he slept.

The saloon had quieted the instant Longarm stepped through the batwings. Even the bar girls turned to look at him, their eyes cold, their sallow faces hard. On all sides of him the bar's patrons froze as well and turned to look him over, their eyes like the bores of sixguns, their mouths hard and unsmiling. More than a few of them reminded Longarm of small, unwholesome beasts. One fellow, his elbows resting behind him on the bar, resembled a pig, with his crushed nose, swollen face, and tiny eyes; another stand-

31

ing by the door had the secret, cunning look of the ferret, with his pointed snout, sloping shoulders and forehead; directly in Longarm's path stood an oversized rat, with his dirty whiskers, protuberant teeth, and round ears. All of them, without exception, were dressed in greasy Levi's, shirts, and vests that after a long winter would have to be peeled off, layer by layer.

They disapproved of him, of course. Despite a light patina of dust that covered his hat and shoulders, Longarm was dressed as neatly and as cleanly as circumstances would allow, in his snuff-brown Stetson, brown tweed britches, and frock coat. He was taller than any of the saloon's patrons as well, and seemed to loom spookily over them, his movements sudden but silent, and as fluid and effortless as an Indian. In short, not only was he a stranger in their midst, but his appearance was a studied insult to their habitual, bone-deep slovenliness.

Ignoring the stares and the questioning glance of the bartender, Longarm headed on down the bar toward the doctor. The rat-faced fellow hesitated for an instant, then stepped aside just enough to let Longarm ease past him. The man smelled of horse manure and obviously needed some teeth removed.

There was an empty chair at the table where the doc was sleeping it off. Longarm sat down and found himself bathed in the man's stale, whiskey-foul breath. As Gurney snored, his mouth hung open wide enough for Longarm to see the deplorable state of his remaining teeth. The doctor looked well past sixty, his face sunken alarmingly, his eyes resting in dark hollows. Dressed in a threadbare black frock coat and jacket, a stained string tie at his throat, the man seemed to have almost no physical substance, reminding Longarm of a conservatively dressed scarecrow with most of the straw missing.

Though reluctant to awaken the obviously exhausted man, Longarm reached over and tapped him lightly on his wrist. It took a second tap to make the man quit snoring,

32

and a third to get his eyes open. Shaking his head to rid it of the last webs of sleep, Doc Gurney straightened in his chair, blinked owlishly at Longarm, then moistened his dry lips.

"You rang, sir?" he inquired mildly, his voice surprisingly resonant.

Longarm smiled. "Sorry to wake you, Doc. Got a few questions."

"No questions before a libation, friend. One cannot get blood from a stone, nor clear answers from a dry palate. Join me in a drink, sir."

"Of course."

The doc waved at a sullen, alarmingly buxom bar girl. She pulled herself away from her beer-swilling companion only reluctantly and looked at Longarm, not the doctor, when she reached their table. Doc Gurney had obviously overextended his bar tab.

"Maryland rye, straight," Longarm told the girl, then glanced at the doctor.

"A fine selection," said the doctor. "You are, sir, a man after my own heart." He winked broadly at the girl. "Charity, my dumpling, would you make that a double, please?"

The girl left. The doctor leaned forward on the table. "Now, sir. What seems to be ailing you? Piles, perhaps? A common complaint, sir."

As Longarm tried to protest, the doctor silenced him with a wave of his parchment-skinned hand.

"Now, don't be embarrassed, friend," he said. "This particular affliction comes from sitting too long in the saddle, aggravated by too many beans and an excessive consumption of black coffee. Or is it, perchance, something more serious?" He tipped his head and waited for Longarm's response.

"It's not me I'm worried about, Doc."

"That so?"

Their drinks arrived. The doctor farted gallantly as the girl planted his double in front of him. Then he winked

33

broadly across the table at Longarm and lifted his glass in a salute. Longarm barely had time to return the salute before the doctor was slapping his empty glass back down upon the table. "So who are you worried about, mister, if not for yourself?" he asked.

"Brad Tarnell."

The doctor's amiability vanished. "May I ask your business, sir?"

"I'm a lawman. Custis Long, deputy U.S. marshal. If you know where Brad Tarnell is, Doc, I'd appreciate you telling me right now."

"I don't dare, Marshal. I value my life."

"You've seen him recently—on business?"

"You might say that."

"Well, that bullet you dug out of his thigh—I put it there."

The man's wrinkled prune of a face twisted into a wry smile. "I did find it hard to believe that Brad shot himself cleaning his gun. I never heard of Brad cleaning anything."

"Where is he?"

"Can't tell you, Marshal. As I said before, I value my life. Not only that, but my livelihood depends on my ability to patch the wounded bodies that find their way to this weathered slab of a town, without revealing to the authorities the whereabouts or the names of any of my patients. Perhaps you fail to realize where you are, sir."

"I'm in Pine Tree City."

"True enough. But have you any idea what the function of this deplorable pile of boards really is—up here so far from the new frontiers out West, tucked away in this bucolic farming and ranching community?"

Longarm shook his head, not because he wasn't beginning to realize what kind of a hellhole Pine Tree City was, but because he wanted to hear the doctor tell him. The man sounded like someone who knew how to use words, and Longarm always admired a man who could do that convincingly.

34

"This is where the bad ones come to lick their wounds, Marshal—or divvy up their ill-gotten gains, or find new recruits for their nefarious schemes. A few miles west of here is the Badlands. As mean a stretch of country as ever I've clapped eyes on. Don't let the grass and the trees and the lazy streams fool you. There's hidden canyons and small valleys tucked safely away in the hills. This is dangerous country, Marshal—especially for the likes of you."

"If you don't tell me where Brad Tarnell and his brother are holing up, this saloon will become a very dangerous place for you, Doc."

"You are threatening me?"

"I am."

"You are a lawman, sworn to uphold the law. You would not descend to bullying a man who has sworn to heal the sick, tend the wounded, and comfort the afflicted—no matter what crimes the poor bastards might have committed."

"Yours is a noble cause, Doc, but I'm in a hurry, and those men tried to bushwhack me."

"Then you do plan to bully me?"

"Yes," Longarm replied mildly.

"There's no way I can talk you out of it?"

"No way, Doc. I'm sorry."

"Ah, well. Then so be it. Before you begin your deplorable bullying, could I trouble you for another drink?"

"Of course. Maryland rye? Double?"

"That would be fine."

Longarm waved over Charity, gave her their order, then turned back to the doctor. "Well?"

"I am not sure I will be doing you a favor, Marshal. If you insist on finding Brad and his brother, you'll end up with considerably more than you bargained for, I assure you. You're just one man, after all."

"You let me worry about that."

"You're bullying me again, Marshal."

"So I am."

Their drinks arrived. Doc Gurney downed his second

35

double even faster than the first, wiped his mouth with the back of his hand, and leaned closer to Longarm. "Wolf Hollow. A ranch at the head of it. You'll find a grievously wounded Brad Tarnell holed up there with his brother and the remnants of a gang that has vowed to even the score with you. The Lavery clan is soon to join them, I understand."

Longarm finished his drink and chuckled. Doc Gurney had known all along why he was so anxious to find the Tarnells. "Thank you, Doc. I promise they'll never know how I found them. Now how do I get there?"

"There's a rutted trail heading west out of Pine Tree City. Stay on it until you come to the Badlands, then go north to Saddle Butte. You'll find a creek leading from it. Follow the creek into the Badlands until you come to a pine bluff. Keep going, along the base of the bluff, south for about three miles. You'll see a break in the wall. Follow it into Wolf Hollow. Then pray your luck holds. It has been doing uncommonly well for you, so far."

"Thanks, Doc."

As Longarm turned to get up, he saw a tall, rugged blond man of about forty years enter the saloon. He was greeted by many of the saloon's patrons before he joined a few men seated around a large table along the wall. The men at the table had obviously been waiting for him. The blond fellow's face and something about his walk were surprisingly familiar, though Longarm knew he had never seen the man before.

"Who's that hombre just came in, Doc?"

"Matt Swenson."

"He have a daughter?"

"That he has, indeed. And a right pretty bundle she is, for a fact." Gurney looked shrewdly at Longarm. "From what little I gleaned from the wild babblings of Brad Tarnell, you not only know Matt's daughter, you owe her considerable."

"That's right, Doc. I do. You think Tarnell might take

36

after the girl for what she did?"

"Nope. They expect trouble from Matt's daughter whenever they tangle with her, and they don't want any trouble from Matt. Not now, they don't."

"Did Brad Tarnell do any babbling about the reason for him trying to bushwhack me?"

"No, he didn't, Marshal. He was in no condition to make any sense, and I was too busy plucking lead from his thigh to bother with whether he made sense or not."

Longarm stood up. "Then I'll have to ask him myself."

"You'd better hurry up, then. I don't give Brad much of a chance. He lost considerable blood."

"Then I'll ask his brother."

He nodded goodbye to the doc and started from the saloon. Before he reached the door, Matt Swenson and the men he had joined earlier got to their feet and preceded Longarm out through the batwings. They were quiet and purposeful as they mounted up swiftly and rode out of town, a rooster-tail of dust marking their swift departure.

It was getting close to sundown and Longarm had put in a full day. He ducked back slightly as a drunk spun out through the batwings and pirouetted past him into the street; then he started for the hotel he had passed earlier.

The sound of gunfire in the street below woke the tall lawman. He got swiftly out of bed and padded on bare feet to the window, his .44 in his right fist. There were no streetlamps in this relic of a town, but from the light escaping from the four saloons down the street, Longarm saw the two riders sweeping down the street from the corner, tossing lead into the night sky as they rode. Hell-raisers, celebrating their drunk as they rode out of town. Longarm watched them sweep past the hotel; then, with a weary shrug, he turned back to his bed.

He never reached it.

Through the door burst two men, guns blazing as they rushed at the bed, unaware in the dim light that Longarm

37

had left his bed and was standing in the shadows by the window. The walls of the small hotel room seemed to hurl the shattering detonations back at Longarm with redoubled fury, as the room filled quickly with powder smoke. Longarm swung up his Colt and fired through the gloom at the two men, his double-action Colt jumping in his hand like something alive. The two men buckled and tried to turn. Longarm fired twice more, carefully this time, and knocked both men backward onto his riddled bed.

The thunder in the room faded. As Longarm lit the lamp on the bedside table, he heard a faint scream of alarm from someone in a room down the hall. A moment later he heard footsteps on the stairs. Longarm watched as the desk clerk plunged into the room and pulled up before the two bodies sprawled on Longarm's bed. The clerk spun to face Longarm.

"I had two visitors," Longarm told the old man. "Did you let them past the desk?"

"No . . . no, sir," the clerk said. "I didn't."

"Who are they?"

The fellow peered more closely down at the two men sprawled on their backs. In the light that shone in through the open doorway, Longarm thought one of the men looked vaguely familiar, even though he was certain he had never seen him before.

"Them's the Lavery brothers, mister. You done killed them. Both!"

"I didn't have much choice. Is there any law in this town?"

The clerk looked wide-eyed at Longarm. "No, sir. We . . . we got a real quiet town. We don't need any law."

"Until tonight," Longarm corrected him.

The man nodded dully, then turned to look back down at the two brothers. Yes, they were familiar. The family resemblance to the two men Longarm had buried earlier that day was quite pronounced.

"I want a new room. And the next time I suggest you

38

be a little more careful who you let past you. Is that clear, mister?"

The fellow swallowed unhappily and nodded. He understood—perfectly.

# Chapter 4

The desk clerk found Longarm a room farther down the hall. Once the clerk had pulled the door shut behind him, Longarm proceeded to drag his mattress off the bed and over to the wall beside the window. He was sitting up on the mattress, reloading in the dim light filtering in through the window, when someone knocked softly but firmly on his door.

Leveling the gun at the door, Longarm called wearily, "Come on in. The party's just beginning."

The door was pushed open, and into the dark, moonlit room stepped an older woman of considerable heft. She was dressed in a long, rose-colored, satiny nightgown. Though she was wearing a nightcap, her long hair—still gold, but streaked with gray—had been combed out so that it flowed well past her shoulders and down her back. Even in the dim light, Longarm could see that she had been a handsome woman in her day and could still turn a few heads if she had a mind to do so.

When she saw the bare, gleaming bedsprings in the dim light, she looked startled. Glancing swiftly around, she caught sight of Longarm squatting on the mattress by the window, his sixgun pointing at her. Instantly, her confusion turned to outrage.

41

"Put that cannon down, mister, or I'll have you thrown out of this hotel! I am an unarmed woman, and I did not come here to be threatened!"

"I wasn't expecting you, ma'am," said Longarm, dropping the Colt into his holster beside him on the floor. "I've had a bad night, you see. Cowboys shooting up the town as they ride out, then two damn fools blundering into my room and ventilating my mattress. You can understand my bein' a mite spooked."

As he said all this, he got casually to his feet. He had pulled on his britches and boots before leaving the other room, but he was not wearing a shirt. She looked at him for a long moment, noting his build and the way he stood before her, and seemed to like what she saw. Her anger faded. She took a deep breath, and smiled.

"I heard about your tribulations, mister," she said. "This is my hotel, and I have come to offer you some help."

"All the help I need, ma'am, is a good night's sleep."

"Well, you won't get that if those Laverys have any friends. And I am afraid, mister, that they do."

"What's your offer?"

"Come downstairs to my suite. As my guest, you'll be perfectly safe."

"That's right neighborly of you, ma'am, but ain't that going to raise hell with your reputation?"

"Never had one to worry about, mister. Not in my line of work, if you get my meaning. I've retired this past year, but everyone in this town knows where I got the money to buy this hotel. Everybody knows, and nobody cares."

"And you're sure I'll be safer down there than on this mattress?"

"Safer and a damn sight more comfortable."

"You're on, ma'am. I thank you kindly, and if you'll wait just a minute, I'll get my possibles and follow down after you."

"I'll wait."

It didn't take but a minute or so for Longarm to replace the mattress on the bed, grab his gear, and follow after the

42

woman as she led him down the stairs to her suite alongside the front desk. One of two doors behind the desk opened into her suite, and as Longarm followed her into it, she turned, closed the door, and introduced herself.

"My name's Beverly," she said, "and you'd be Custis Long, U.S. deputy marshal."

"You got it all, Beverly. I see you've been talking to Doc Gurney."

She nodded. "After the doc looked over those two bodies and pronounced them officially dead, he told me about his conversation with you in the Cowboy's Palace. You've pretty near wiped out the whole Lavery clan, Marshal—and that makes you a marked man in these parts. That's when I decided to invite you to sleep down here."

"Don't tell me why. Let me guess. You've always had a soft spot in your heart for lawmen."

She shrugged. "I admit that's not very likely. But it's late. We both need our sleep. We can talk more in the morning." She smiled, lifted the kerosene lamp off the small table by the door, and started through the living room to her bedroom. "You can sleep in bed with me, or on the sofa in here."

"Would I hurt your feelings, Beverly, if I chose the sofa?"

"Not at all. I figured, from the look of you, that you would refuse my invitation. Besides, even though I'm retired, giving it away still seems to go against the grain with me. Old habits die hard. I'm sure you undersatnd."

"Never having been in that line of work, I find it a mite difficult, but like you say, we can talk more in the morning."

Once Longarm was curled up comfortably on the sofa, he heard Beverly begin to snore. He buried his head in a pillow and congratulated himself on his wisdom in turning down Beverly's invitation. He would never have gotten to sleep alongside that awesome series of detonations.

Breakfast was brought to them by a thin, solemn blonde girl not much older than sixteen. Longarm and Beverly ate

43

it in a cozy nook that looked out through a modest bay window at the backside of Pine Tree City. Outhouses, emptying into sluggish ditches that led down to the stream beyond a ridge, were the first structures the bright morning sun turned to gold; the ancient, weathered face of the bluff overlooking the town was the next.

Beverly saw his sardonic gaze and laughed softly, her opulent figure jiggling slightly. Despite her size, she had a surprisingly pretty face, and her long hair, still combed out, had much to do with that. They had finished their first coffee and both of them were finishing off the breakfast with their second cup. "Not much of a view, I admit," she said. "But the other side is no better. Horses' tails swinging at tie rails. Whiskey-sotted no-goods with guns, sitting on their asses, planning schemes that will lead them and fools like them to a mean death." She sighed and smiled wearily at Longarm. "I am afraid I much prefer the outhouses and that bluff."

"Would you care to tell me why you settled in Pine Tree City in the first place?" Longarm asked. "And even more important, why you decided to befriend a man of the law in a rat's nest like this?"

"I told you last night we'd have time to talk, and I guess this is that time," she said.

Beverly leaned back to allow the blonde girl to clear off their small table, then waited until the girl had left before beginning her story. Born and brought up in Connecticut, Beverly and her younger sister, Anne, had a quiet, almost idyllic childhood until tragedy struck. Their mother had died of scarlet fever. Their father—a skilled engraver—was unable to deal with the tragedy. He began to drink and lost his job. Debt soon made them destitute and at last their father fled to the West, promising to return with enough money to pay off their debts and rescue them from their mother's parents, Calvinists who never tired of reminding them of their father's disgrace.

But of course Beverly's father never returned to Connecticut. At last, unable to stand her grandparents any

44

longer and having heard from a mutual acquaintance that her father had been seen in Minnesota, Beverly set out to find him. The trail led eventually to Pine Tree City, after which it dried up completely, and Beverly, her funds exhausted, was forced to find work. Her comely physical appearance and the dearth of any respectable employment led her inevitably into the oldest profession. She saved her money, in keeping with her Calvinist upbringing, and was soon able to run her own house as well as send money back to Connecticut for her sister's education at various fashionable finishing schools.

After working as a nurse for a while, Anne married a Calvinist acquaintance of her grandparents. The marriage was a disaster and Beverly's sister ran off to join her in Pine Tree City. Fortunately, by the time Anne reached the place, Beverly had invested everything in this hotel, so that her sister was not forced to visit her in a bawdy house. Still, it was soon obvious to Anne what profession it was that had kept her in those expensive finishing schools. Shocked, angry, she ran off again, this time determined to find her father where Beverly had failed.

"I don't like Anne very much," said Longarm.

"Nevertheless, I would like you to do what you can to find her, Marshal. She's a wild, headstrong girl, alone in an unfriendly land. The fact that she is my sister might help her with some of these hardcases, but with others it might be disastrous. I fear not only for her life. She could lose far more than that."

"I see what you mean."

"Will you help me?"

"What makes you think I can? I have other business in this place."

"Yes, I am sure you do. But I believe you owe me something. Those two you shot upstairs were not the only men in this town looking for you last night."

"I see. Doc Gurney told you that too, did he?"

"Yes, he did."

"I think I'd like a talk with him. Soon."

45

"That might prove interesting, I am sure. But, as I said just now, you owe me. It was only because you were under the protection of this suite, you might say, that you survived the night in Pine Tree City."

"Why should these hardcases have any more respect for you than for anybody else?"

"I wish I knew, Marshal. But it is true. Ever since I came to this town I have felt it—a sense that I need not worry, that these men would not harm me. And I have not been mistaken. I have seen it on their faces and noticed it in their manner. These men approach me only with respect."

"Strange."

"Yes, but I do not question it. I always treated the men who came to my house—or to my bed—with respect and kindness, no matter how difficult that became at times. I suppose this is the way they repay me."

"That's as it may be, Beverly, but it's a mite hard to believe."

She shrugged. "Will you help me?"

"Maybe we can help each other."

"Fair enough."

Longarm took out of his wallet the list containing the numbers of the federal notes that had been stolen from the Northfield bank by the James gang and handed them to Beverly. "If you or your clerks would keep a list of these numbers by your cash drawer, I would appreciate knowing who, if anyone, passes any federal reserve notes carrying these numbers."

"You're looking for bank robbers, are you, Marshal?"

"Yes." Longarm had no intention of telling Beverly any more than that. Besides, she might have burst into whoops of laughter if Longarm had let on that it was the James gang who had stolen those notes and that it was, in fact, the elusive—and now legendary—Jesse James that Longarm was in Pine Tree City hoping to track down.

"I'll do it, Marshal. And you'll help me find Anne?"

"Tell me what you can about her. I'll be moving into the Badlands soon, and I'll keep an eye out for her. I'll ask

46

some questions. That's the best I can offer."

Beverly sighed and finished her coffee. "I guess that will have to be it, then." She pushed herself to her feet. "I have a picture of her and I can give you a pretty good description of the horse she was riding and the clothes she wore."

"And if you'll give me that list back, I'll make copies of the numbers."

"I have a desk over there," Beverly said. "You can make the copies while I get the pictures." She handed the list back to him and left the room.

With a sigh, Longarm walked over to the desk and sat down to copy the list. He had little hope that he would be able to find Beverly's sister, or that if he did, what he found would make Beverly very happy. A lone girl from the East with a strict Calvinist upbringing didn't stand much of a chance in this part of the world.

The hump of Saddle Butte loomed above the dark hills of the Badlands just ahead of Longarm as he topped a rise close to sundown that same day. He reined in his black to let the animal blow, and glimpsed far below him—at least a mile distant—seven freight wagons crawling through the narrow green belt bordering the creek Doc Gurney had told him to follow into the Badlands.

He decided he would join the teamsters. They would be camping soon and perhaps one of them might have spotted Beverly's sister during his travels. It was a long shot and Longarm was not counting very heavily on it, but it was worth a try, he figured, as he angled his black down the slope.

He had not ridden far when he saw a swarm of riders sweep out of a cottonwood grove just ahead of the freight wagons. The unmistakable pop of distant gunfire came to Longarm clearly. At once he put his horse to a gallop, snaking his Winchester out of its boot as he did so. The battle far below him was a short one, as the teamsters put up little resistance to the gang surounding them.

It was not until Longarm reached the flat and started

47

racing across it toward the creek that he was spotted by the highwaymen. Two riders detached themselves from the main body, rode into the shallow creek, splashed across it, then began galloping warily toward Longarm. Then the lead rider had his Colt up. Longarm dropped the reins of his hard-charging horse and dug his heals in as he lifted his Winchester to his shoulder. The lead rider fired at Longarm— smoke puffing back from the muzzle an instant before the sound of the report.

It was a nervous, hasty shot that went wild, but it served to begin the proceedings. Longarm held his rifle easily, allowing the uneven motion of his mount to bring up the sights. When he caught the lead rider's face, and then the man's shirtfront, in his front sight, he stroked the trigger. The rifle kicked against his shoulder; for a moment the two riders ahead of him were obscured in smoke, and then, as the smoke whipped on past him, he saw the outlaw pitching backward off his horse, his hat flying.

The second rider yanked his horse to a sudden, cruel halt and flung himself from his saddle, taking his rifle with him. Kneeling beside his fallen companion, he levered a fresh cartridge into his firing chamber and aimed at the onrushing lawman. Longarm fired first. The outlaw's hat snapped back off his head. Coolly, the outlaw drew a bead on Longarm and fired. The puff of smoke and the report came at almost the same time.

Longarm was in the act of levering a fresh cartridge into his chamber when the bullet caught the rifle's stock, shattered it, and flung it out of Longarm's hand. The impact caused Longarm to loose his balance momentarily. He grabbed for the reins, missed, and fell heavily forward onto the horse's neck. The sudden shifting of his weight caused the already laboring black to stumble. The animal tried to gather his legs under him, but he was too far gone by this time—and went down, flinging Longarm over his neck to the ground.

Longarm came down hard and remembered thinking the

48

ground was soft enough as he continued to roll over—when the back of his head slammed sharply down upon the projecting face of a rock embedded in the ground. It felt as if a blacksmith's hammer had struck him, the way his head rang. The light in the sky above him seemed to brighten, then dim ominously. Though he was fully conscious, he found himself unable to move a muscle. He felt the ground under him shudder as horses pounded closer; then the dim sky was shut out by a circle of grim riders.

Longarm found it impossible to focus his eyes. And though the ring of faces peering down at him from under wide hatbrims faded ominously whenever the throbbing in his head intensified, he was able to make out four men in all. One of them was Matt Swenson. They were discussing him, and as they did so, a few of them laughed meanly. It had the sound of coyotes barking over a meal. Longarm had difficulty catching their words, however, above the roaring in his ears. He saw the man he had shot leaning painfully over his pommel to stare balefully down at him, his cheek distended with chewing tobacco, a bloody patch covering his right shoulder. He said something to Matt Swenson, then directed a dark plume of tobacco juice at Longarm's prostrate form. The heavy wad struck the ground close by Longarm's right cheek, splattering it. The laughter that broke from the ring of riders came to him clearly enough then—despite his fogged senses.

Matt Swenson took out his sixgun and aimed carefully at Longarm. Perfectly aware that Swenson was about to administer the *coup de grace*, Longarm tried to close his eyes. He was unable to do so, however, as the gun bucked in Swenson's hand and a second titanic hammer crashed down upon Longarm's skull. Longarm felt his head drive deeper into the ground. All light winked out. He had the absurd sense that the earth had opened up beneath him and that he was falling through it—all the way to China.

49

# Chapter 5

Longarm opened his eyes and saw nothing.

He refused to panic, however, despite the smell of raw earth and damp, rotting timbers that hung heavy over him. He lay perfectly still and waited, the sound of his heart pounding in his chest comforting him somewhat. At least he was not dead. He might be buried alive, but he was not dead. Then he heard the cool rush of a mountain stream nearby, and birdsong echoing in a meadow below him. He closed his eyes and relaxed, then slowly raised his right hand to his head and felt the heavy swath of bandages wound tightly about it.

Abruptly, a door was flung open and a blinding shaft of sunlight exploded into the small cabin. Longarm closed his eyes convulsively against the sudden brightness and turned his head away, but not before he glimpsed the bent, squat figure of an old man entering the cabin. His eyes still closed, he heard footsteps approaching his cot.

"Awake, are you?" the old man asked, bending over Longarm. The fellow smelled of rancid buckskin, unwashed hair and feet, and chewing tobacco. His stench would have

51

prompted a saloon to close early.

Longarm turned his head back around and found himself looking up at a red-bearded oldtimer whose head seemed to have been screwed onto his shoulders as a halfhearted afterthought. "That's right. I'm awake, old man. Who might you be?"

"The redskins used to call me Crooked Elk." The old man had bright blue eyes that blinked down at Longarm with the clarity and innocence of a child. "You can call me Ike. That's what most white folks call me."

"Most obliged, Ike, for the accommodations. You wouldn't happen to know what day this is, would you?"

The old man squinted and turned his head slightly, his entire torso moving slightly with it. "Reckon it's either Thursday or Friday. Then again, it might already be Saturday. Don't keep much track of days, mister—just the seasons, and they've been coming at me faster each year." He chuckled. "You're a lawman. I saw your badge. Custis Long, you is. I found you near the creek along with a dead teamster. Got myself a mule out of it too. You was still alive, so I brung you back with me."

"The horse I was riding? It was a black."

"Found it grazing half a mile further up the creek."

"You brought it back with you?"

"Yup. I flung you over the saddle. No way I was going to carry you myself."

"Much obliged."

"You had some folding money and some silver. I took that too. Winter's comin' on an' I'll need provisions."

"You're welcome to most of it, but I'll need some. As soon as I get out of this here fix, I've got some riding to do."

The man grinned, revealing a mouthful of blackened stumps. "You'd be after gettin' even, huh, for them that done you in?"

"That's part of it."

Longarm reached out, placed his hand against the wall

52

beside the cot, and pushed himself to a sitting position. His head spun sickeningly for a moment. When it had steadied, he swung his legs off the cot and rested his bare feet on the cabin's dirt floor.

"My boots," Longarm said. "I'll be needing them too, if you don't mind."

The old man shrugged. "Well, I must admit, they fit me real tight, but I had my eyes on 'em, that I did, and that frock coat of yours too. Nice material. Can't blame a man for lookin' ahead," he said, turning and shambling over to a corner into which most of Longarm's clothes had been thrown.

Longarm allowed himself an ironic chuckle as Ike, somewhat reluctantly, brought him his clothes. He almost felt sorry for the old man's loss, almost sheepish that his continued existence had, in a sense, robbed the man of a needed addition to his wardrobe.

When Longarm had awakened to find himself in Ike's cabin, it had been late in the afternoon. As soon as he found he had apparently been unconscious for two full days, he tried to hasten his recovery by checking out the condition of his black and then exploring the wild country about Ike's cabin. He nearly overdid it. A sudden attack of dizziness prompted him to sit heavily on the ground and lean his back against a sapling. Ike had told him that his head wound consisted of a deep gash. The bullet fired by Matt Swenson had not penetrated his skull, but it had certainly registered a mean enough blow. The result, as Longarm realized, had been a severe concussion. Now, peering about him at the gathering dusk and doing his best to ignore the deep throbbing inside his head, he derived little comfort from Ike's claim that Longarm's thick head of hair would soon cover completely the long gash in his scalp.

Ike found him at length and hunkered awkwardly down beside him to tell him supper was ready—muskrat stew, made rich on this special occasion by generous helpings of

53

the last of his potatoes. Longarm thanked Ike and told him he'd like to rest a few minutes longer.

Ike understood that and sat down beside Longarm to wait with him. The oldtimer obviously enjoyed the company of a fellow human. As the throbbing in Longarm's head diminished, he took out two cheroots and a sulfur match, and handed one of the cigars to Ike. Longarm lit his own and Ike's cheroot, then leaned back and inhaled deeply. For a while the two smoked in silence.

"What happened, Ike?" Longarm asked eventually. "I mean to your head. The way you hold it."

"Grizzly," Ike said, puffing contentedly.

"There's no grizzly in these parts."

"I know that. Didn't happen in these peaceful, Eastern parts. Out West in the Tetons. Used to trap there before the curse of civilization overtook it. Came back to my camp one bright October afternoon and found a grizzly in my tent, tearing up a storm. Had already ruined a passel of beaver skins, so I wasn't as careful as I might have been. I went in after it. My rifle misfired. The grizzly swiped at me and his claw took out a chunk of my neck and shoulder, mauled me some, then dragged me a ways before he lost interest." He chuckled. "I think it was my smell saved me."

"You're lucky to be alive."

"That I am. When I could move, I figured out the only way I could stem the bleeding and heal the wound was tip my head over and lift my shoulder to close up the wound. Then I bound up my head and shoulder like that. It stopped the bleeding all right, and the wound closed. But that meant I couldn't straighten my head again, less'n I wanted to rip open the wound again."

"So you were one of them Mountain Men."

"Yup, and don't you believe half of what them children tell you." He smiled. "'Cept what I just told you, of course." He took the cheroot out of his mouth and spat. "That's the truth. I got the twisted body to prove it. After that, I figured the only animal could kill me would be the human variety."

54

There was no response Longarm could make to that beyond agreeing. The old Mountain Man was undoubtedly correct. The Most Dangerous Animal was the two-legged variety, all right.

"How you feeling now?" Ike asked, getting crookedly to his feet. "That there muskrat stew is probably getting cool by now. And I wouldn't like to see that. It'll do you some good if you take it piping hot."

"I'm fine," Longarm said.

He got carefully to his feet and began to stride gingerly along beside the crooked oldtimer.

The two men ate in front of the cabin at a deal table Ike dragged out for the occasion. The swift stream rushing past the cabin made pleasant enough music, but the flies and mosquitoes were a nuisance. It would have taken a lot more than that, however, to detract from the savory magnificence of Ike's muskrat stew. Large, surprisingly sweet chunks of muskrat swam in a thick broth alongside potatoes, some tender greens the old man had gathered, and wild onions. Ike need not have worried about the stew cooling off any. The onions took care of that. The stew brought sweat to Longarm's brow, a feeling of deep contentment to his belly, and an almost miraculous cessation of his pounding headache.

During the meal, Ike explained how he had been on hand to help Longarm in the first place. It seemed that he had long been a student of Matt Swenson and his gang. They prowled the fringes of the Badlands, preying on the freight wagons that hauled bonded goods on their way from St. Paul to the Canadian border and on into Canada. Swenson never highjacked an entire shipment, just those items he could sell at a profit to those American merchants unwilling to pay the high American tariffs—items such as Swiss watch movements, machine tools, cut gems, and so on.

Matt Swenson did not attack every freight wagon that moved north, only those that contained the type of compact goods he could sell easily to willing merchants. As a result, the gang would often leave other items lying about in the

55

wake of their attacks. It was Ike's habit, therefore, to trail these wagon trains once they reached the outskirts of the Badlands, in hopes that Matt Swenson would attack, after which, of course, Ike could pick up the leavings.

"You done spoiled things for everybody this last time, Longarm," Ike said, his blue eyes twinkling.

"How so?"

"Matt's gang looks fearsome enough, tearing out of the woods and shooting off pistols in the air, but they are real careful never to shoot any of the teamsters. And when Matt takes what he's looking for, he lets the wagon go on its way. This time, with that foolhardy charge of yours across that flat, everything went to hell. One of the teamsters got brave and had a shootout with one of Matt's men, and during your short battle, the rest of the teamsters hightailed it out of there. Matt never got what he wanted, and this time the teamsters will have a bloodier story to tell."

"Up till now, you mean, Matt's been playing it pretty close to the chest."

"That's the way I see it." Ike took the cheroot Longarm offered him and lit up. "He must have Beazley and a few of the other sheriffs in his back pocket. He's been around, Matt has, and he's served his time. He's trying to keep this operation of his as quiet as possible. He don't want to stir up no hornet's nest." Ike chuckled. "Hell, the merchants is glad enough to get the goods Matt brings them. If they had to pay them high tariffs, they'd go out of business."

"Any merchants in particular?"

"There's one in Northfield. Wiggins. He owns the Wiggins Emporium. Never did like the bastard. Wouldn't give his best friend credit."

"Who's the go-between?"

"What makes you think I know?" Ike asked craftily.

Longarm didn't reply, just waited patiently.

"I figure it's Welland, the bank cashier. I seen him meeting with Matt once in a while out here, generally after a wagon train's been looted."

56

"Welland is dead."

Ike was surprised to hear that, and when Longarm identified the culprits as the Tarnell gang, Ike nodded sagely.

"Makes sense. Them two gangs've been at each other's throats for some time now. Frank Tarnell sees what a nice deal Matt has, and wants in. That would make sense, all right."

Longarm was reminded then of Randy's remark about her father being one of the Last Great Western Bandits. "So now Matt will have to lay low for a while. Is that it?"

Ike spat. "Reckon that's so. Which means the pickin's is goin' to be mighty lean for a spell."

"You got a mule this time."

"And one body I had to bury."

"I'm glad it wasn't two."

"You ain't told me what you're doing in these parts."

Longarm wondered if it would be safe to tell Ike why he had been heading into the Badlands. It might be safe, he concluded, but not really very wise. He shrugged. "Let's just say I've been sent out here to look things over. After all you've just told me, you can understand that, can't you?"

"Sure, I can understand that. And your mother didn't raise you up to be no flannelmouth, neither."

Longarm leaned back. He was aware suddenly of just how exhausted he was. He had only been up and about for a few hours, but it was enough, obviously, to remind him of how mean a concussion he had sustained. Ike saw the look on Longarm's face and suggested he might want to go back into the cabin and rest up on the cot.

Longarm did not argue with the man.

A strange scratching sound on the door awakened Longarm. He sat up on the cot and reached under his pillow for his Colt. As he was doing this, the scratching sound came again. Ike, who had been sleeping on the floor in deference to Longarm, got to his feet and hurried to the door. Pulling it open, he stepped back as something wild and gibbering

57

swept into the cabin. Ike lit a candle and Longarm was astonished to see that the wild animal Ike had just let into his cabin was a woman.

Her dark hair was wild, matted, her face streaked with dirt. There were scratches on her cheeks and forehead. What remained of her bodice was barely enough to cover her breasts. Her skirt had been ripped so badly that her legs, from the knees down, were exposed. She was barefoot, and under the dress she wore no chemise or corset. Her exposed limbs and shoulders were a mass of ugly bruises, and as she crouched in the middle of the room, like a cornered wild thing, Longarm saw that once she had been pretty enough; but in her eyes now all he saw was mindless terror, the terror of any wild animal tormented beyond its ability to understand.

As Longarm put down his Colt, the girl, uttering a tiny cry, rushed at him. Before he could stop her, her fingers began undoing the bandage that still covered his head wound. Her strength was formidable, and Longarm had to struggle to grab her wrists and hold her back. For a moment her face was distorted with a kind of wild confusion at his actions, and then—just as swiftly—her face brightened and she shrank back, tipping her head to look at him almost proudly.

"Leave her be, Longarm," Ike told him. "She's just tryin' to help."

"Help? For God's sake, Ike. You must be as crazy as she is."

"I don't know about that. After all, she's the one who bandaged that head of yours in the first place."

"Her?"

"That's right."

"Jesus," Longarm said softly.

The girl approached him again, less frenetically this time. As she put her hands up to his head to continue unraveling the bandage, Longarm made no effort to stop her. The smell of her was not pleasant, and he could not

58

look closely at her bruised, tormented body without wincing inwardly. But when she stepped back, his bloody, unraveled bandage piled high in her arms, he caught something in her face that jogged his memory.

Before he could speak to her, she snatched up a water bucket by the door and vanished out the door. Longarm followed after her to the door and saw her down on one knee by the stream as she dipped the bucket into the running water. She was going to wash off his head wound, Longarm realized. In the bright moonlight, she looked almost wraith-like as she bent over the bucket. Longarm had difficulty believing in the reality of all this.

"You better explain that slowly to me, Ike," Longarm said. "Who is this wild woman, anyway?"

"She belongs to Tarnell's gang, I reckon. Every now and then she busts loose and turns up here. I feed her, gentle her down if I can, before they come after her."

"And she was here when you came back with me before?"

"That's right. You was out cold, or you'd remember. When she calms down, she acts almost human. I suspicion she was a nurse one time, the way she cleaned out that wound of yours and bandaged it, gibberin' all the while she did it."

"Then what happened?"

"One of Tarnell's gang came for her."

"You didn't protest?"

"I never have—whenever they come after her. I know my place in these Badlands, Longarm. Besides, if I'd've put up a fuss this last time, they might have found you here. If that'd happened, you never would've woke up, and I'd likely be dead too. This here stretch of the Badlands is Tarnell's private kingdom, pilgrim. He don't take kindly to squatters. He lets me along b'cause he figures I'm harmless."

The girl straightened, tugging at the full bucket with both hands, and turned about to return to the cabin. As

59

Longarm watched, a rider swept across the moonlit meadow below the stream, splashed through it, and reached down for the girl. She dropped the heavy bucket, the water spilling from it, and tried to fight the rider off. But she was no match for him, and was swept up onto the pommel of the rider's saddle.

By this time Ike had crowded Longarm out of the doorway, not at all gently. The rider, with the struggling girl firmly in hand, spurred his horse up to the cabin door.

"We got a party tonight, Ike," cried the rider. "We need our chantoosey!" He laughed coldly, meanly. "No sense in invitin' you, though. You're way past the age. But next time, we'd sure appreciate it if you could give her a bath."

With a bark of laughter, the rider swung his horse brutally about and galloped off, the moonlight catching the spray of water erupting under his mount's hooves as he splashed through the creek.

Slowly, Ike closed the door. Longarm went back to the cot and bent over to lift his bedroll out from under it. In a moment he took a faded picture out of an oilskin packet and, without a word, handed it to Ike. The old man took the picture over to the guttering candle and squinted at it carefully.

"Is that her, do you think?" Longarm asked.

Ike took a while before answering, then handed back the picture. "Might be," he said. "Yessir, it might be. Same round face, eyes, mouth. 'Course, you can't really tell for sure. The girl in that picture was sure dressed a lot better than that poor wild devil we just saw."

"How long has this girl been around?"

"About six months, I'd reckon. But I don't expect she's goin' to last another six. She gets crazier and wilder ever' time I see her. It sure is a mean and terrible thing they's doin' to her, and that's a fact. They remind me of some Indians I once tangled with. Only there was an excuse for the way some Indians treated a white woman—they didn't know no better."

60

"What's she called?"

"I don't know."

"What can you tell me about this gang, Ike? How come they're holed up in these Badlands?"

Ike raised his eyebrows as though surprised the answer wasn't self-evident. "Why, them boys is runnin' a hideout ranch. Any desperado on the run from a peace officer can light out to Wolf Holler and hole up until the heat lets up. I hear tell they got bank robbers, train robbers, cattle rustlers—all kinds of bandits using Wolf Holler at one time or another. Hell, who'd think to look in Minnesota for 'em? 'Course, Tarnell makes 'em pay for the privilege, and then when things begin to cool off, the men drift into Pine Tree City to make their plans. Real neat, Longarm. And I wouldn't've told you a thing about it if that girl hadn't showed up just now. I tell you, it's gettin' to me, seeing her like that."

"What can you tell me about the gang members?" Longarm asked.

Ike sighed. "There's one that acts real strange."

"How so?"

"Well, he never leaves the holler. Stays there all the time, though he rides about the Badlands on occasion. But it ain't just that. There's something *about* him."

"Can't you be a little more specific, Ike?"

"Once, his horse went lame and he stopped by here to borry a mule from me to get back to the holler. All the while I was saddlin' up my mule for him, he kept hisself in the shadows. It was on toward evening, anyway, and he didn't have much trouble keeping out of my sight. I couldn't be sure, but I thought he kept a black bandanna wrapped tight about his face. I couldn't be sure because his frock coat had a wide collar and he kept the collar up all the time he was here."

"Did he pay you for the use of your mule?"

"Yes, he did. And right generous he was, too."

"Who else is there?"

61

"Finn Tucker, Loomis Leach, Steve, Lem, and Tip Wilcox."

"Tip Wilcox is dead."

"How's that?"

"I killed him. He was part of the gang that killed Paul Welland and then ambushed me."

"Well, then. I guess you can forget about Tip. But if I was you, I'd be a mite leery of bumping into Steve and Lem."

"Who else is there?"

"You know about Frank and Brad Tarnell."

"Yes, I do. Brad's got a bad wound in his thigh."

"You give it to him?"

Longarm nodded.

Ike sighed. "Well, then. There's the Laverys, Red and Tim, and two others, just as wild."

Longarm decided he wouldn't tell Ike that he had already had a run-in with the Lavery brothers. "That's it, then?"

"Quite an army, I'd say. And a bad outfit, Longarm. Cruelest bunch I've ever come across. I'd sooner deal with Apaches on the warpath than with them hombres. They're mean clear to their bones."

"I'll be careful."

"You'd better be."

Longarm felt of his head wound. It had scabbed over cleanly and there was not too much tenderness around its edges. It had not become septic, he realized. Thanks to that crazy woman. Thanks to Beverly's sister, Anne.

Carefully, he placed the picture Beverly had given him back in the oilskin pocket, then replaced his bedroll under the cot and slumped down on it, staring at the closed door, going over in his mind carefully all that Ike had just told him. A cruel, sadistic bunch they had to be to turn a young girl into what Longarm had just seen crouching before him in the light from Ike's flickering candle.

He took a deep breath. He was still too weak to do much good now, but he wasn't going to waste any more time

62

if he could help it. He had been wondering if he should go after Matt Swenson or investigate further the gang at Wolf Hollow.

The wild thing that had entered Ike's cabin a few moments before had made that decision for him.

# Chapter 6

At first, Longarm could not be sure. But as the rider climbed the trail a few yards below the timbered ridge upon which Longarm was crouching, there was no longer any doubt. The rider was Frank Tarnell. Behind him rode another rider Longarm did not recognize—a sharp-featured fellow with pale, almost white eyes.

And behind them came a riderless horse led by the second rider. Tied down securely on its back was a soogan obviously containing the body of a dead man. Longarm had led enough horses similarly laden into town to recognize the load—and the somber errand it implied.

Frank Tarnell was journeying into Pine Tree City to bury his brother.

As soon as the two riders were out of sight, Longarm led his horse farther along the ridge into Wolf Hollow. Not long afterwards, he found himself in sight of the ranch buildings Doc Gurney had described. They were well below him, tucked neatly against the base of the bluff, the compound shaded by cottonwoods. Longarm moved back off the ridge and tied his horse to a sapling in a well-watered grove where there was plenty of fresh grass. Then he returned to the ridge and followed it until he found a secure vantage point above and behind the ranch buildings. He made himself comfortable and waited.

65

There were at least ten horses in the corral behind the main barn, but Longarm did not see anyone until approximately an hour later when Anne was dragged from a shed behind the main cabin by the same fellow who had taken her from Ike's place three days earlier. He flung her unceremoniously through the cabin's door and followed her in. Not long after, woodsmoke began pulsing from the chimney as Anne began preparing supper for her captors.

About a half-hour later, a tall, lean fellow left a building across the compound and started toward the cabin. This fellow reminded Longarm of the dude Ike had described to him as being unwilling to show himself. Though the man's hatbrim shielded most of his features, Longarm thought he caught the tight flutter of a bandanna covering the lower portion of his face. Not long after the dude entered the cabin, five other men left a bunkhouse and straggled across the compound toward the cabin also, passing a flask among them as they went. It was obvious from the way some of them staggered and the raucous cries they emitted that they were not drinking water. As the five of them piled into the cabin a moment later, Longarm left his vantage point and found a level spot well back from the rim.

He was exhausted and realized he was still suffering from the aftereffects of his concussion. Closing his eyes, he went over in his mind what he planned to do. It was simple, really. He would let the men drink themselves into a stupor, and then go down there and see what he could do about bringing out Anne.

There was still a chance, of course, that the James brothers had simply not shown themselves yet. At any rate, none of those six men he had just seen resembled either Jesse or Frank; and the more Longarm pondered on it, the more unlikely it seemed to him that he would find either of the James boys hiding out in the ranch below him.

When the moon was high and the uproar coming from within the cabin had subsided appreciably, Longarm darted

66

from the corral fence to the rear of the cabin. Flattening himself against the log side, he moved cautiously along it until he reached a window and peered in. The view from where he was standing was a disappointment. All he could see was the back of a chair, a table with a lamp on it, and a corner of a woodstove. He was pulling back from the window when he heard from just behind him the sound of iron clearing leather. He spun about swiftly, then raised his hands—just as quickly.

The cowboy who had the drop on him was smiling. In the darkness, all Longarm could make out was the man's broad grin and his bright, amused eyes. His sombrero was resting across his back, hanging from the cord around his neck.

"Well, now, looky here," the man said, thrusting the muzzle of a huge Remington revolver into Longarm's belly. "We got a visitor!" The man's smile vanished, and leaning close, he growled, "What the hell you doin' here, mister? Tell me before I blow a hole in your gut!"

"I heard tell there was a place in these hills where a man could lay low from the law. Ain't this the place?"

"It sure enough is. What you runnin' from, mister?"

"Take that cannon out of my gut, and I'll tell you."

The fellow drove the muzzle in about an inch deeper and smiled again. "Tell me anyway, friend."

"Embezzlement."

"Shit!" the man exploded. "I thought you was gonna say you committed a *crime*. You're just a sneak thief. We don't have no truck with sneak thieves here. Get on out of here before I spank you!"

The window beside Longarm was flung open and someone stuck his head out. "What the hell you got out there, Buck?"

"An embezzler, he says! Lookin' for a place to hide. I told him this ain't no place for the likes of him."

"My horse is gone," Longarm told the fellow in the window. "I'm beat."

67

"Bring the poor son of a bitch in," said the man in the window. "I never have seen an embezzler up close."

The fellow called Buck removed the muzzle of the Remington from Longarm's midriff and motioned with it, indicating that Longarm should go ahead of him around to the front of the cabin. "And don't try nothin', mister," said Buck, "or I'll kick you in the ass!"

Buck was still filled with mirth as he shoved Longarm into the cabin and closed the door behind them. Holstering his gun, he grinned around at the cabin's occupants. "See what I find out there when I go to take a shit?" It was obvious that Buck regarded Longarm's sudden appearance as a welcome break in the monotony of the place.

Looking quickly about, Longarm saw two men asleep on the cot, one sprawled awkwardly on top of the other. They looked as if a cannon going off under the cot would not be enough to awaken either of them. Three men were sitting at a table playing poker, one of them the fellow with a bandanna covering the lower portion of his face. The fourth man, the one who had called from the window, was the same man who had taken Anne back from Ike's place and who had earlier dragged Anne across the compound.

Anne was standing in an open doorway that led into a bedroom. She was staring fixedly at Longarm. Then, with an inarticulate cry, she ran at him, arms outstretched.

"Catch her, Finn!" cried one of the men at the table.

Finn, the one who was evidently Anne's keeper, darted swiftly forward and intercepted the girl. He was not gentle with her as he pulled her swiftly around, slapped her hard, then hurled her back toward the bedroom. "Get in there, damn you!" he cried.

Anne reeled back against the doorjamb, the back of her head slamming it hard. She slid, dazed, to the floor. The men laughed at the way she sprawled, her legs spread wide, very little of her hidden from their gaze. Longarm held himself in check, but only with difficulty.

Finn turned back to look up at Longarm. "What's your name?"

68

"Percival Barrows," Longarm said in as subdued a tone as he could manage.

"Percival!" Finn roared. "Percival! Oh, my! Look what we have here!"

"I told you," said Buck. "We got ourselves a real prize. He's a sneak thief looking for a place to hide."

"All right, Percy," said Finn. "How much you got with you? This place don't come cheap, you know."

"I don't have a cent."

"You what?"

"I spent all the funds I embezzled."

"On a woman, I'll wager," said the dude at the table.

"Why, yes, as a matter of fact. That is unfortunately true."

"Listen to the man, will you?" said Buck, chuckling.

"You can't stay here, Percy," said Finn coldly.

"Unfortunately," said the dude, getting to his feet and walking closer, "you can't leave, either. Someone like you—a rank amateur, obviously, without much practical skill as an outlaw—is liable to talk too much about this place." Pulling up in front of Longarm, he glanced sideways at Buck. "I suggest you take the man's weapon, Buck."

Buck stepped forward, flipped back Longarm's frock coat, and removed Longarm's Colt from his holster. As Buck did so, he noted with a frown the workmanship that had gone into Longarm's cross-draw rig. "Where the hell did you get that rig, Percy?" he asked, suddenly suspicious. "It don't look like something a bank clerk would invest in."

Longarm smiled. "That's what the bank inspector said when I suggested he let me examine it. He was quite surprised when I turned his gun on him and locked him in the vault."

"Perhaps you have some promise, after all, Percy," said Buck. He looked at the dude. "What do you think, Cal?"

The dude pulled the bandanna down off his face. Longarm had all he could do not to react. It looked as if someone had raked a pitchfork back and forth across the man's cheeks. His lips were pitiful scars. "Perhaps we had better

69

wait for Frank to get back. Let him decide what to do with this tenderfoot." He frowned and looked closely at Longarm. "If that is indeed what he is."

"Where'll we put him?"

"In the back shed."

"A prison?" Longarm asked, apparently mildly upset. "You are going to incarcerate me? I came here to escape such a fate."

"Maybe you did," said Cal, "or maybe you had other reasons. You simply do not look as stupid as you would have us believe you are, Percy."

"Let's go, Percy," said Buck. "I'll show you to your . . . quarters."

This brought appropriate laughter from the two men at the table and a smile from Cal and Finn. As Longarm left the cabin with Buck, he glanced back and saw Anne, still sprawled on the floor. But she was no longer unconscious and was watching him closely.

In fact, Longarm was almost certain he had caught a faint gleam of hope in her demented eyes.

Buck took Longarm to a storeroom in the same building across the compound from which Longarm had watched Cal emerge earlier that evening. As Buck unlocked the padlock and pushed the door open, Longarm got a strong whiff of fresh paper, printer's ink, and a fainter odor of machine oil. He was reminded fleetingly of a print shop or newspaper. As Buck started to push him into the lightless room, Longarm pulled up and turned to face Buck.

"Say, what caused that fellow's face to be all scarred up like that, Buck?" he asked.

"You mean Cal?" Buck grinned suddenly. "A pretty horrible sight, wasn't it? He likes to pull that bandanna down on people to get their reaction. You didn't react much, but I could tell you almost shit your pants, all the same."

"But what happened to him?"

"Oh, he told us an apprentice of his in Minneapolis got

70

himself in a dander about something and threw acid in his face."

"Buck, are you on the dodge? Is that why you're here?"

Buck snorted derisively. "You think I'd be here if I could be somewhere else?"

"How much did you have to pay?"

"A pretty sum, I can tell you. They took all the gold and silver I had and paid me back in paper money—but not full value, that's for damn sure. And they kept the difference."

"They kept the difference?"

"Sure. That's what it's costing me to hole up here."

"Say, listen, Buck. You seem like a decent sort. If it's money these fellows want, what about this valuable watch I'm wearing? Solid gold, it is. If I let you have it, maybe you could bring it to Cal and the others to show them I'm willing to pay my share."

In the darkness, Buck had difficulty seeing the watch that Longarm pulled out of his vest pocket. As he leaned closer, Longarm lifted out the watch fob in order to give Buck the watch to take over to the cabin. Buck stuck his sixgun back into his holster and reached out for the heavy watch, a conspiratorial smile on his face.

That was when he saw the derringer's muzzle staring up at him from Longarm's right hand.

"Jesus," Buck muttered, stepping back and raising both hands, "Cal was right, damnit!"

Longarm stepped swiftly closer to Buck, slipped the man's sixgun out of its holster, then took his Colt from Buck's belt and stuck it back into his own cross-draw rig. "Step into that storeroom, Buck," Longarm said quietly, covering the outlaw with his own Remington.

Without a word of protest, Buck stepped inside. Longarm sighted a lantern, handed Buck a match, and told him to light it. Buck lit the lantern. Longarm took it from him and placed it high on a shelf so that it would give him a better view of the room's contents.

He saw boxes of paper, gallon cans of printer's ink, and

71

a small but gleaming press in the corner. The press was obviously finding a great deal of employment in this hideaway. And it was obviously not printing a newspaper. Longarm looked at Buck. "Acid, you say. Someone threw acid in Cal's face."

"That's what he told us, Percy."

Longarm smiled at Buck. "My name's not Percy."

Buck nodded resignedly. "I didn't think it was."

"Turn around, Buck."

The man did as he was told, but with great reluctance. Longarm stepped swiftly closer to Buck and brought the barrel of the outlaw's gun down on the crown of his head. Buck sagged forward onto the floor, striking it facefirst, and lay perfectly still. Longarm leaned close to make sure the man was unconscious, holding the Remington on him just in case. Buck was out cold.

Longarm took the man's keys, stepped out of the storeroom, locked the door, then hurried back through the darkness toward the cabin. Buck's weapon was a single-action, but Longarm was going to need all the firepower he could muster, once the element of surprise was gone.

At the rear of the cabin he peered into the bedroom window.

What he saw appalled him. Cal and Finn Tucker were having their way with the struggling Anne. Her wrists were tied to the bedposts at the head of the bed, her ankles to the bedposts at the foot of the bed. She was naked, the sickly white flesh of her malnourished body glistening with sweat and discolored from its many ugly bruises. To keep her screams from disturbing those in the other room, they had stuffed a dirty towel into her mouth. Nevertheless, Longarm was able to hear her faint gasps of despair and loathing as the two men took their turns.

The window was not down all the way, and the two were too busy to notice Longarm slowly pushing the window up. The only light came through the partially open door. Holding Buck's sixgun on the two men, Longarm eased one leg

72

over the window frame, and then pulled himself into the room. Cal, in the act of pulling up his britches, turned as Longarm rose to his full height. Before he could utter a sound, however, Longarm brought Buck's big Remington around, catching the man on the left cheekbone. The force of the blow was enough to fling the man violently back against the door, slamming it shut.

Ribald shouts came from the other room. The men playing cards were amused at the troubles Cal and Finn were having subduing Anne. One of the men shouted for them not to be greedy, to leave some for him.

Finn was in an awkward position. Busy with Anne, he had not turned when he heard Cal slam the door. But he was curious enough to slow down somewhat and start to turn his head. Longarm did not let him finish. He brought the gun barrel down on the top of Finn's head with all the force he could muster.

Grunting explosively, Finn collapsed facedown on Anne's writhing body. With a bitter, silent oath, Longarm grabbed the man's shoulder and flung him bodily off Anne to the floor. Again, laughter erupted from the other room, this time followed by the sound of a man getting to his feet. Longarm heard heavy footsteps approaching the door.

Swiftly, Longarm stepped behind the door and waited.

Someone at the table called to this third fellow, reminding him he had a game to finish. The fellow paused at the door, turned, and went back to the table. "Hurry up in there," he called above the sound of his chair scraping back into place. "I want to get mine before Buck gets back. You know how goddamn long he takes."

Longarm looked down at the pitiful figure still twisting before him on the bed. Then he bent and untied both of Anne's ankles. At once she tried to turn her body away from him. He then untied one of her wrists. She began to rip at the towel in her mouth. Longarm leaned over her and held the wrist firmly and shook his head. But she would not heed him. She tried to claw his eyes out. Reluctantly,

73

Longarm leaned closer and punched her flush on the jaw. It was a measured blow that knocked her unconscious without really hurting her.

He finished untying her, snatched her torn garments off the floor, then dropped her lightly ahead of him out the window. With her flung over his shoulder, Longarm raced through the night toward the horse barn. Saddling one horse for her in the darkness, he mounted it, rode out of the barn with Anne—still unconscious—draped over the pommel, then galloped swiftly past the cabin. The thunder of his mount's hooves brought two men to the cabin doorway.

Aiming carefully as he rode past, Longarm fired at them. He saw one man pitch forward into the yellow light spilling from the door as his companion ducked back inside.

As Longarm galloped through the moonlit hollow, he reminded himself that this was not why Billy Vail had sent him to this place. He was supposed to be looking for Jesse and Frank James—and failing that, he was expected at least to trace those stolen federal reserve notes. Instead, he was working for an ex-madam, rescuing her sister from a clutch of degenerates.

Still, he could not work up a sweat about it. There was no way he could have left this poor mad creature with those men. Billy Vail could not really find it in his heart to disagree with Longarm's decision.

The problem now was not Billy Vail anyway, Longarm mused as he cut up a steep incline, heading for the ridge above, where he had left his black. The difficulties he faced at the moment held a more immediate and pressing concern for him, chief among them being how he was going to spirit away through the darkness a madwoman who, once she regained consciousness, would begin screaming bloody murder, alerting the entire countryside to their whereabouts. How could he keep on slugging her unconscious?

And then he thought of Ike. Perhaps the old man would

74

be able to calm her down enough so that Longarm could bring her through the Badlands quietly. In addition, he might perhaps have something more decent for her to wear than the ragged dress that now covered the girl's pathetic nakedness so poorly.

Just as his mount pulled up onto the ridge, he heard the pounding of hooves below him in the night. The chase was on.

# Chapter 7

Longarm had some difficulty finding his horse. By the time he did, the Badlands on all sides of him seemed to echo with shouts and the thunder of many hooves as the irate outlaws scoured the hollow and then climbed to the ridge to continue their search.

Anne regained consciousness not long after two horsemen charged past them in the dark. Longarm had dismounted and pulled the two horses into a grove as soon as he heard them coming. Anne had been draped over the pommel of his saddle, and as the riders disappeared into the darkness ahead of them, along the ridge, she began to struggle and slid awkwardly off his horse. Before Longarm could reach her side, she began to scream.

He clamped a hand over her mouth. She managed to bite his palm. He pulled his hand back swiftly and slapped her, very hard. Her face snapped around under the force of his blow. Again he placed a hand over her mouth and, leaning close, tried to talk to her.

"Anne, I'm trying to help you!" he pleaded. "I want to take you back to Beverly!"

She did not seem to hear him and began kicking out at him with her bare feet. The damage to Longarm was negligible, however, and after she had struck his boots twice with her right foot, she subsided somewhat, moaning softly

77

as she slumped back down onto the ground. She began to rock painfully, holding onto her foot.

Slowly, carefully, Longarm took his hand from her mouth. The moaning was louder, but Longarm judged that the sound of it would not carry far, and straightened. She was still naked. He reached into his blanket roll where he had stashed her pathetically inadequate dress and handed it to her. Still favoring her foot slightly, she stood up and dropped the dress over herself. Pleased at his progress, Longarm turned to bring closer the horse he had taken for her. She would have to ride astride, but she should be able to manage that somehow, he imagined, as he grabbed the horse's reins and pulled it closer.

When he turned back to Anne, she was gone.

He hadn't heard a sound. He swore and peered into the darkness about him and caught a glimpse of something white vanishing up the trail along the ridge. He raced after her. Twice he stumbled in the darkness. But at last he managed to bring her into sight less than a mile farther on. She was heading for a campfire, he saw to his horror.

Then she fell, heavily. He heard her muffled cry of pain. Closing on her as she lay sprawled beside the trail in the darkness, he saw the two figures huddled around the campfire get to their feet and peer in their direction. At once Longarm dove to the ground, scrambled a few feet farther to Anne's side, and then, with one terrible swipe, caught her about the neck and dragged her close. Before she could cry out, he had clamped his right hand over her mouth. With the other, he held her neck—tightly.

Her eyes bulged in terror. He leaned close. In a fierce, exasperated whisper, he said, "I don't want to hurt you, Anne! I just want to take you back to your sister! Away from those men!"

It did not seem to make any sense to her. She struggled desperately to get free of him. He knew he could not hold her much longer, and yet he could not increase the pressure on her neck.

78

"We're going to see Ike," he told her. "Ike!"

At once she calmed. For perhaps the first time she looked at him with eyes no longer wild with fear. She seemed to recognize him at last, as she had when he had first entered the outlaw's cabin. Her struggling ceased and Longarm took his hand from around her neck, though he did not dare take his right hand from over her mouth.

She stiffened abruptly, her eyes suddenly filled with panic once again. Longarm followed her terrified gaze and saw that the two outlaws he had glimpsed standing by their campfire were now quite close, their pistols out as they moved carefully through the night toward them. They had heard enough to know that something was afoot and were coming to investigate.

Longarm dragged Anne across the ground to a clump of juniper and took out his Colt and waited. He had been forced to switch hands when he drew his Colt, so that it was his left that now covered Anne's mouth. She began another furious struggle to pull herself away from him. He leaned close to her.

"Do you want to go back with them?" he whispered fiercely.

She looked up at him, wide-eyed. Her struggling ceased abruptly.

Longarm turned his attention back to the approaching outlaws. He recognized them. They were the two men who had stayed at the table during Longarm's brief visit to the cabin. The moonlight fell over them like a bright blue mantle, but the tops of their faces were hidden completely by the shadows of their hatbrims, so that only their chins and moustaches were visible. And the sixguns gleaming dully in their hands. They passed without comment over the spot where Longarm and Anne had struggled a moment before, kept going for a few hundred feet farther on, then turned back around, no longer as wary, and walked back to their campfire, holstering their guns as they went.

Before they reached their campfire, five riders boiled out

79

of the darkness beyond it and swiftly dismounted. The two men ran to join them, and as Longarm watched a moment later, the seven outlaws rode off down the trail.

Longarm got slowly to his feet, dragging Anne up with him. As the riders disappeared into the darkness, Longarm turned to Anne. "If I take my hand away from your mouth, will you keep quiet?"

She nodded fiercely.

He removed his hand. She smiled at him, and what came from her mouth then was more hair-raising than if she had screamed. It was a laugh, or rather a low, seductive chuckle. She moved closer to him and thrust her little body against his, her mindless laughter curdling Longarm's stomach. As her skinny arms twined themselves around his neck, she began to speak softly to him.

But her words were worse than the laughter. They expressed a mindless catalogue of filth. A steady stream of foul images poured from her lips. He felt the hair rising on the back of his neck as he attempted to pull away from the girl. Suddenly furious, she began clawing at his face. He managed to catch her wrists and bend them until she was forced onto her knees before him.

She stopped struggling, flung herself at his feet, and wrapped both arms around them, moaning hysterically. Then she began to cry. Painful, wracking sobs broke from her frail body.

Longarm patiently unwound her arms from around his legs and, lifting her in his arms, began to carry her back the way they had come. By the time he reached the waiting horses, Anne was asleep. Unwilling to awaken her, he mounted up carefully with her still in his arms and, leading the horse he had taken for her, rode on through the night.

At daybreak he found a secluded spot under an overhanging ledge that offered enough water and grass for the horses. He was still some distance from Ike's cabin and did not want to take the chance of approaching the place in daylight. The gang members were obviously familiar with it and with

80

Anne's propensity for seeking refuge there.

Anne seemed closer to unconsciousness than to sleep. It was almost as if she had been drugged. She did not protest when he settled her on his bedroll close in under the cliff and left her to keep a lookout. The ledge gave him a spectacular view of the eastern reaches of the Badlands and of the rolling, wooded countryside beyond.

Close to ten that morning, he caught sight of dust being raised far below him. Watching closely, he eventually picked out two riders. They were pushing their mounts hard and were coming from beyond the Badlands, from the direction of Pine Tree City. As the two riders passed below him and out of sight, Longarm recognized Frank Tarnell and the rider who had been with him earlier when they rode into Pine Tree City to bury Brad. That dismal business had been tended to, it appeared, and Frank was now anxious to rejoin his cohorts in Wolf Hollow. The man was in for a surprise when he got there.

Longarm went back to check on Anne, then returned to his lookout post. Around noon, Cal and Finn Tucker and the other cardplayer galloped into sight, heading for Wolf Hollow also. The three riders were abusing their horses pitifully. They were coming from the direction of Ike's place, and Longarm did not like the look of things. He kept watch for the remainder of the afternoon, dozing once or twice.

Around sundown he went back to Anne and woke her.

She came awake startled, wild-eyed. He gentled her as best he could with a comforting hand on her arm. She calmed down quickly, then reached out to him. It took a moment for him to realize that she was reaching for the wound on the side of his head, which she had treated earlier. He took off his hat and bent his head so she could see it.

Her fingers played lightly along the length of the scabbed-over gash, wonderingly. Abruptly, she looked at him, puzzled, then about her—as if she were finally awakening from a long nightmare.

"Ike," he told her gently. "We're going to see Ike now."

81

She nodded.

He looked at her closely. "You all right now, Anne? You won't be screaming out anymore?"

For a moment she seemed to consider his question; and then, as if she had pulled window blinds down before her eyes, there was no longer any expression left in them. Her face grew tight. Her mouth trembled. Slowly, tentatively, the tip of her tongue showed in one corner of her mouth. Abruptly she smiled at him, seductively, evilly.

"Oh, damn!" Longarm muttered. Then he spoke sharply, angrily: "Stop that nonsense, Anne. You're just playacting!"

She came at him then, a wild thing, ferocious, clawing for his eyes. For a moment or two Longarm tried to reason with her. But she heard nothing and once or twice almost broke through his parrying arms. Reluctantly, Longarm measured her carefully and slapped her as hard as he dared on the side of her face. She was unconscious before she struck the ground. As he lifted her a moment later onto the back of his horse, he remembered reading somewhere about the way people in the Middle Ages cured the insane: they threw them into snake pits.

The trouble was that someone had already done that to Anne.

Dusk was shading into night as they approached Ike's place. Longarm's apprehension had been growing since earlier that afternoon when he had seen those three riders coming from this direction, and for the past half-hour he had been aware of the smell of woodsmoke heavy on the wind. It was too pervasive a smell to be coming from a chimney, and there was an ominous feel to it.

A surprisingly docile Anne was riding behind Longarm when they broke finally into the clearing that fronted Ike's cabin. Only one wall and a few crossbeams remained of it. Its burning embers were still glowing like devils' eyes in the gathering dusk. Longarm heard Anne's tiny cry and

82

looked back to see her throw herself from her horse. Before he could dismount to stop her, she was racing toward the shell of what had once been Ike's cabin. As the girl splashed across the narrow stream, Longarm spurred his horse after her and overtook her in front of the cabin.

As he flung himself from his horse, she made no effort to evade him. He caught her about the shoulders and spun her around to keep her from rushing into the still-smoking wreckage. She screamed then, loudly, piercingly—and pulled away from him, pointing up at something hanging in the smoke-filled dusk behind him.

He turned and saw Ike—hanging by a thick rope looped over a charred cross-beam. There was little left of the old man that was still recognizable—except for the unmistakable twist of his head. He had been hung up in the midst of the fire and roasted alive. Strips of blackened skin hung from his naked torso like ribbons of tar. His eyes were black, burnt-out, empty sockets, and yet they seemed to be staring at both of them, pleadingly:

*Get me down. For Christ's sake, get me down.*

Anne slumped to the ground and began rocking back and forth. Longarm left her and plunged into the smoking rubble. Glancing up at the body, he despaired of finding a way of reaching high enough to cut the rope that secured Ike to the beam. Then, with an angry snarl of frustration, he grabbed one of Ike's scorched ankles and yanked on it as hard as he could. The scorched rope gave way and the old man came down in pieces—and Longarm found himself with a handful of soapy flesh.

After burying Ike, Longarm continued on through the night to Pine Tree City. A stone-faced Anne rode beside him without a glance to the right or to the left. The shock of seeing Ike like that and her grief at the old man's death were perfectly understandable to Longarm. He had expected wild, uncontrollable behavior as a result; but instead of

83

carrying on, she had simply continued to rock quietly back and forth, uttering not a word. When he was ready at last to move on, he had found her still sitting on the ground where she had slumped earlier, as silent as a stump, and had been forced to pull her to her feet and then lift her into the saddle, bending her arms and legs the way a child would a doll's limbs to make it sit up.

It was curious, Longarm reflected. Anne appeared to be able to understand much of what happened about her, and to react almost normally at times. Then, without warning, she would go wild. Or, as she was doing at the moment, she was capable of lapsing into an impenetrable silence that shut out the world completely. Longarm wondered if she had not somehow found a way to block out all those events she did not want to experience. It would be nice, he concluded, if she could do that, especially if it meant she might be able to block out the horror of these past months in Wolf Hollow—and the terrible sight of old Ike hanging from that beam. . . .

It was not long after this inward musing that the dark buildings of Pine Tree City loomed ahead of him on the horizon. It was only a few hours before dawn, so that even the saloons were dark and silent. He rode up the main street, past the four corners, watching Anne out of the corner of his eye to catch any hint that she recognized the place.

But there was nothing to indicate that she even knew she was in a town.

Longarm rode behind the hotel and dismounted at the rear door. He left Anne on her horse, mounted the small porch's steps, and knocked. There was no response, so he knocked a second time, louder. It still took a while for a light to show in Beverly's ground-floor suite. A dark form appeared at the bay window, peering out at him. A moment later the rear door was pulled open and Beverly rushed out onto the porch in her robe, a cry of pure joy bursting from her as she saw Anne.

It caught in her throat, however, when her eyes grew

accustomed to the darkness and she was able to see her sister more clearly.

"Anne!" Beverly cried. "What's wrong! My God! What have they done to you?"

She rushed past Longarm down the steps, and reached up to help Anne off the horse. There was no response from Anne, none at all. She did not turn to look down at her sister. She did not, in fact, move a muscle. Her eyes just stared fixedly ahead of her at the wall of the hotel. Longarm stepped down off the porch, reached past Beverly, and gently pulled Anne from the horse; then, holding her gently in his arms, he carried her up the porch steps and into the hotel, a distraught Beverly right behind him.

"Take her into my bedroom," Beverly told Longarm, as she closed the door to her suite.

Longarm nodded and continued through the living room and into Beverly's bedroom. It was with some difficulty that he was able to straighten Anne's limbs sufficiently to get her comfortable on the bed—not that the silent girl complained.

Standing back then, Longarm looked down at Anne and shook his head at the amazing—and troubling—transformation that had come over the girl since they had reached Ike's place and discovered what the outlaws had done to the old man.

What he had been mulling over earlier, he realized, must have been right on target. Seeing Ike like that had been the last straw for Anne. She wanted no more of this nightmare and was deliberately blocking it all out, everthing—even the sight of her sister. She could not take a chance with what life could do to her any longer—she did not dare. What little sanity she had left was huddling deep inside of her, too terrified to look out ever again.

Beverly rushed into the bedroom then, took one shuddering look at her sister, then shooed him from the room. Longarm left the hotel and brought the horses to the stable. He woke up the one-legged hostler in the process, paid him

85

liberally for his interrupted sleep, and returned to the hotel. A deeply troubled Beverly was sitting at the table in the bay window, two steaming cups of black coffee before her.

Longarm sat down beside Beverly at the table and gratefully pulled one of the cups toward him.

"Longarm," said Beverly, her voice hushed, "what's happened to her? She just lies there. She's all bruises. She must have lost twenty pounds. And that dress she was wearing! It's the same one she rode out in!"

Longarm placed his hand gently over hers for a moment. "I don't know all of it, Beverly. But I'll tell you what I can. Do you have any whiskey to go with this coffee? I think we could both use some."

She nodded, got up, and returned a moment later with a fifth of rye. Longarm took it from her and poured generous dollops into both cups, and began his story.

Beverly was weeping silently, tears rolling down her cheeks, by the time Longarm completed his account. He had long since finished his coffee. He leaned back wearily in his chair.

"What can I do, Longarm?" Beverly asked. "Is she completely insane now?"

"She's been through too much, I'd say. What she needs now is care. I reckon there's a chance she'll come around, if she really wants to. But it will take time. I've heard of cases like this—when the Indians took white women captive and used them too harshly. Some of them were never the same again, even long after they were recaptured and restored to their families. But some did snap out of it. It just took time and lots of patience."

A deep, troubled sigh issued from the big woman beside Longarm. She brushed the tears out of her eyes. "Well, I've got the time, I guess. And I'll just have to have the patience."

Longarm patted her hand encouragingly. "Good. Maybe it'll be all Anne needs. I'd say she put up quite a battle before she *did* crack."

86

"What are your plans now, Longarm?"

"Shut-eye. Then I'm returning to Northfield. Did anyone pass any bills with those serial numbers I gave you?"

She shook her head.

"Did you see Frank Tarnell while he was in town burying his brother?"

"Yes. He stayed here in the hotel."

"I'd like to see any bills he might have passed."

"He paid in silver, Longarm. He always does."

Longarm nodded. "Has there been anyone else, any strangers, just in from the west maybe, and looking for a place to hide?"

"Not that I know of, Longarm. The girls didn't mention anyone."

Longarm nodded and stood wearily. "Can I borrow that sofa of yours again tonight, Beverly?"

"Of course."

Not long after, with Beverly moving quietly into the bedroom to join her sister, and with his Colt tucked under his pillow, Longarm fell into a deep but troubled sleep.

He did not awake until late the next day, too late to start out for Northfield. He imposed on Beverly's hospitality for a second night and left Pine Tree City the next day. Not until the following morning did he reach Randy's farmhouse.

He called out, "Hello, the farm!" as he rode into the yard, but there was no response. Longarm pulled up and listened. He could hear the clucking of chickens from the hen coop and the sound of animals stirring restlessly in the barn. Yet no sound came from the farmhouse. As he dismounted, he called out a second time. But again there was no answer. He moved around to the back porch and carefully mounted the rickety steps.

The kitchen was an untidy mess, not at all as Randy had kept it. Deeply troubled now, Longarm went into her bedroom. He winced. Everything he saw was mute testimony

87

to a fierce struggle. The sheer curtains had been ripped from the windows. The bedspread had been soiled and was bunched in a tangled heap at the foot of the bed. Everything that Randy had placed so neatly and carefully on the top of her dresser had been flung with one brutal swipe to the floor. Her box of face powder had burst open, covering the floor with a pale patina covered with bootprints. And in one far corner the music box lay shattered, the tiny sprite on its lid ground into the floorboards.

As he looked down at that once-dancing sprite, an involuntary shudder caused him to glance away and hurry out of the room and back into the kitchen. Randy was gone. This might have happened after she had left, when the house was empty. Drifters could have found the place unoccupied and vented their fury at finding no woman to ravage or money to steal.

But even as he told himself this, he knew it was unlikely. Randy had been here. She had put up a bitter but futile battle, and had then been abducted. Or worse.

Sorely troubled, Longarm left the house, mounted up, and turned his horse in the direction of Northfield.

88

# Chapter 8

Sheriff Beazley was so fat that even his jowls had jowls.

He was sitting in his swivel chair at the moment, leaning far back, his enormous belly thrust out like a balloon about to burst. Around this barrel of a man hung a gunbelt and holster, the sixgun slung so low that Longarm wondered how the sheriff could walk without tripping over it. Perhaps, Longarm mused to himself, he didn't walk; he rolled. Beazley wore a red cotton shirt under a black, buttonless vest, trousers that must have been tailored by a tentmaker, and a tall, white Stetson. His boots were fashioned from finely tooled cordovan leather. He gave the appearance of a very prosperous county sheriff.

"What can I do for you, Marshal?" asked Beazley, his voice rumbling with a practiced friendliness, while his beady eyes regarded Longarm warily.

Longarm put away his badge. Sheriff Beazley had not suggested that Longarm sit down, though there was a chair by the man's desk. His deputy, a rake-thin fellow with gaunt cheeks and protruding front teeth, regarded Longarm man with undisguised hostility from behind his much smaller desk in the far corner. Longarm had met the deputy on his first visit to Northfield. His name was Tod Wiggins.

"I want your help in organizing a posse, Sheriff," Longarm informed the obese man.

"That so? And when do you need this posse?"

"I'll let you know. I've got to telegraph Denver first. And it might take a while before I get a reply."

"May I ask the purpose of this posse?"

"To clean out a nest of rattlesnakes."

Beazley laughed heartily and glanced at his deputy. Tod Wiggins laughed also, but without the slightest appearance of mirth.

"And you need a posse for that, Marshal? I am astonished. I thought that you federal marshals never needed help."

"This one does, and ain't afraid to admit it."

"You talk of rattlers, Marshal. Surely you jest. There are few, if any, rattlers left in this bucolic community. The plow has chased them all West."

"Not the human variety, Beazley. Haven't you or any of your townsmen wondered what's happened to Paul Welland?"

"Not really, Marshal. I was talking to Phineas Biddle, the bank president, earlier today. He is certain Welland has cut out. And good riddance. The man spent more time in the Daisy Miller than he did in the bank. He was a surly, uncooperative employee, and Phineas is glad he no longer has to contend with him. As a matter of fact, the entire town feels the same way. In his cups, he was a mean, unregenerate bully."

"Then it ain't going to exercise any of you to know that he was murdered the same day I rode out of here—and by the same gang of hardcases I now mean to apprehend."

Beazley looked at Longarm for a moment longer. He seemed to be debating whether or not to tell him to go to hell. At last he sighed and straightened in his chair. It squeaked tightly as the man leaned his elbows on his desk.

"And I am to take your word for all this, Marshal? You saw this gang murder Welland?"

"No, I did not. But it was a reasonable suspicion. And not long after they shot Welland, they attempted to bushwhack me."

90

"Did they now? I see you survived all right."

"Yes, I survived. But three of their gang were not that lucky."

Beazley's eyebrows lifted, in spite of himself. He sighed wearily, aware that he was not going to be able to brush off Longarm's request as easily as he might have hoped. "You realize, I am sure, Marshal, that due process must be observed. No matter how justified your assertions, I'll need to know more than you are telling me now. I cannot simply wave a posse into being without good and substantial evidence that it is needed."

"You'll have that when I get an answer to my telegram."

"How many men do you think you'll need?"

"Five would do right nicely," Longarm said, smiling in a way that gave Beazley pause.

"You are uncommonly optimistic, Marshal," the sheriff finally replied. "I doubt if you will find a single man in this settled community ready to strap on shooting irons and follow you into rattlesnake country—let alone five."

"Do what you can, Sheriff," Longarm told the man as he turned to leave. "Soon as I get word from Denver, I'll get back to you. In the meantime you can be checking out those you think might make proper deputies."

Outside the office, on his way to the railroad depot to send his telegram, Longarm pondered the sheriff's reluctance to cooperate. He wondered if any of it could be linked to the fact that his deputy was a brother to the merchant who might be accepting smuggled goods from Matt Swenson. As soon as he sent his telegram, he decided, he would have a chat with Bill Wiggins.

The Wiggins Emporium was a thriving general store that smelled of newly minted hardware, nails, and barbed wire. Longarm purchased a handful of cheroots and asked the clerk if Bill Wiggins was around. The clerk adjusted his steel-rimmed glasses and told Longarm that at this hour of the afternoon, he would most likely find Mr. Wiggins in the Daisy Miller.

91

Longarm thanked the man, walked down a few blocks, and entered the Daisy Miller Saloon. As he had noticed on his first visit to Northfield, the saloon was a clean, well-managed establishment. The sawdust on the floor was fresh, and the well-fed damsels looking down at the men from their frames on the wall were reasonably well clothed, leaving much, but not all, to the imagination. The big chandelier had not yet been lighted. To his right, as Longarm entered, the long bar was lined with men's backs—the bar-length mirror into which they stared was pink with their reflected faces. At this time of the day, only one faro layout was going. In the back of the place a quiet, intent poker game was in progress, a few citizens watching from a respectful distance. A barkeep was hustling whiskey and beer.

Longarm found a place at the bar and ordered a glass of Maryland rye. The barkeep, a hulking fellow with his black hair parted in the middle and greased down smoothly, pulled back a moment and regarded Longarm with obvious distaste. Everyone at the bar noticed, and Longarm saw one of them nudging his neighbor.

"We got the best whiskey in town, mister," the barkeeper drawled. "And the best beer. So what makes you think we'd carry any of that Maryland swill?"

Longarm reached across the bar with his left hand, grabbed the barkeep's shirt, and yanked the man closer. The barkeep managed to reach under the bar and come up with a mean-looking sawed-off shotgun. With his right hand, Longarm brought the barrel of his Colt down hard on the knuckles of the barkeep's hand. The shotgun clattered onto the bar. With a single swipe, Longarm swept the shotgun off the bar, then pulled the barkeep closer and stuck the muzzle of his .44 under one of his nostrils.

"This here's a double-action, mister," Longarm explained softly. "Now you hustle up some of that Maryland rye I favor or I'll blow your nose for you. And to tell you the truth, the way things have been going for me lately, such a diversion just might do me a world of good."

92

"Judas Priest!" the man bleated, his eyes bugging, his voice a strangled whine. "I done told you what we got! We ain't got no Maryland rye!"

"I'll handle this, Mike," said a quiet feminine voice beside Longarm.

Longarm released the barkeep and turned to find himself looking at a very handsome woman.

"And just who might you be, ma'am?" he asked.

"Daisy Miller. This is my saloon. And just who the hell are you?"

"Maybe you could rustle up some Maryland rye, ma'am. That's been known to loosen my tongue somewhat. And I sure have a bad case of the dries."

She looked at him for a long moment, then shrugged. "I might be able to find a bottle. If you'll follow me to my office."

"Lead the way," Longarm told her.

Holstering his Colt, he nodded to the still-shaken barkeep and followed the owner of the Daisy Miller to her office. As she opened the door for him, he glanced back at the saloon. There was not a man in it who was not watching them. He stepped in past her, turned, and waited for her to close the door.

Daisy Miller was almost as tall as Longarm and had a similar, clean-limbed strength about her. She was wearing a wine-colored dress with a daringly low-cut bodice, her ample breasts swelling luxuriantly up from under her tight corset. Dark auburn curls spilled down about her neck. Her nose was sharp and clean-boned, her chin softly round, but strong. It was her eyes, however, that most impressed Longarm. Set well apart under a handsome brow, they were opalescent in color, their luminous depths alive with flecks of emerald.

"Sit down," Daisy Miller told him. "I'll see what I can do about that thirst of yours for Maryland rye."

Longarm took off his hat, spotted an upholstered chair across from a leather sofa, and sat down in it. Placing his

93

hat on the floor beside it, he glanced around him and noted that Daisy Miller's office also served as her living quarters. Beyond the large desk that dominated the room, he saw a doorway that led into a luxuriously outfitted living room. It was into this room that Daisy vanished, to return a moment later carrying a bright silver tray on which were set a bottle of Maryland rye and a single empty glass.

As she placed the tray down on a table beside his chair, she said, "Will I now be privileged to know the name of the man who has so disrupted my saloon this afternoon—and terrified my barkeep out of a year's growth?"

"Custis Long," he replied with a smile. He poured two fingers of whiskey into the glass, then downed the contents.

She sat down on the sofa across from him and crossed her long legs. He heard the pleasant rustle of her petticoats under her silk skirt. "And what is your business in Northfield, Mr. Long? I have not seen you in my saloon before, that I can recall."

Longarm poured himself another drink and leaned back contentedly. "I am here on federal business, Daisy. I'm a deputy U.S. marshal."

"I should think a lawman would show better judgment than to sweep a loaded shotgun off the bar in a crowded saloon. You could have killed one of my customers—or at least injured someone seriously."

"My apologies, Daisy. As I said, I was uncommonly dry, and that barkeep of yours was not very neighborly."

"You must forgive the man. He is quite churlish at times, I must admit, and does not know how to handle a man with the taste to appreciate good Maryland rye."

"Won't you join me in a glass?"

"No. I prefer to cultivate other vices."

Longarm smiled. "And what might those be?"

"Use your imagination, Marshal."

"My friends call me Longarm."

"Am I to be so honored? How nice."

"Where are you from, Daisy?"

94

"Boston."

"That was before. I mean after."

She smiled. "Culver City."

"And then?"

"Deadwood, Dodge City." She sighed. "And a dozen dusty trail towns after that."

"Well, you've done yourself proud here. The Daisy Miller is a fine saloon."

"Yes. I try to give the place the flavor it requires to give these soft townsmen the feel of the Wild West—though all that has long since passed them by. I am afraid my barkeep still thinks he's tending bar in the Dakotas. But then, he is part of the atmosphere these men seem to crave."

Longarm finished his drink and stood up. "Thank you for the drink, Daisy."

She got up also. "I will instruct Mike to keep the bottle ready for you under the bar."

"I'd appreciate that."

"You wouldn't want to tell me why you are in Northfield, would you, Longarm?"

He reached down for his hat and put it on. "Take too long to tell, I am afraid."

"Of course," she said, smiling. "I understand."

They started for the door. Longarm was acutely aware of Daisy's tall, lithe presence close beside him. Before they reached the door, however, it swung open and in burst one of the men Longarm remembered seeing at the poker table when he came in. He slammed the door shut behind him and stood before the two of them, rocking back and forth in a seething rage. He was as tall as Longarm, but considerably leaner. His face was gaunt, his pale blue eyes wild under blond, beetling eyebrows. From his manner, he should have been drunk. But Longarm knew this was not the case.

"What is the meaning of this, Bill?" Daisy demanded. "Don't you know how to knock?"

Bill licked dry lips. "Damn you," he breathed. "You

95

know why I'm in here—why I didn't knock. There isn't a man in that saloon didn't see you invite this gunslick in here."

"They would all have to have been struck blind not to have seen," Daisy replied icily. "But what's that to you?"

"Every man out there is laughing at me. They're saying my girl is going back to her old profession. You're making me a laughingstock."

"And when they said that, Bill, what was your reply?"

Bill compressed his lips bitterly. "I told them once a whore, always a whore—that's what I told them."

Daisy reached out swiftly and slapped Bill, hard. He took the blow without flinching, then snatched at her hand. He caught her about the wrist and dragged her closer. Longarm could see Daisy wincing as his vicelike grip tightened about her wrist.

"Damn you! Damn you!" he cried, his face contorted with rage.

Unwilling to watch any more of this, Longarm stepped between the two, grabbed Bill's wrist, and twisted up with brutal strength. The man gasped and let go of Daisy's hand.

"All right!" Bill cried. "All right! Take the whore. You can have the faithless bitch! You'll just have to learn to stand in line, mister, like the rest of us!"

Longarm swung on the man and was lucky enough to catch him on the edge of his lantern jaw. Bill spun about and slammed, face forward, into the door, then slid all the way to the floor, his hands just managing to cushion his fall. Striding angrily over to him, Longarm hauled him roughly to his feet and pulled the door open.

The saloon was filled with quiet, expectant men, wolfish grins on their faces as they watched the open doorway. Longarm flung Bill at them. Barely conscious, he struck a chair and reached out to a table for support. It tipped under him and he fell heavily to the floor amid a tangle of chairs and shattering beer glasses. Longarm slammed the door shut and turned to Daisy.

96

She was standing in the middle of the room, her face hidden in her hands, weeping softly. He approached her quietly, took her by the shoulders, and guided her gently back to the sofa. Without saying a word, he poured a stiff drink of rye into her glass and handed it to her.

She took it without a word and downed it in one swift gulp. Coughing slightly, she looked up at him through eyes still swimming in tears. "I guess whiskey still has its uses, Longarm."

He nodded. "Guess maybe it does, at that."

"Excuse me," she said, getting swiftly to her feet.

Sitting back down in the armchair, he removed his hat again and watched as she strode to the door and flung it open. Longarm heard the saloon quiet down expectantly at her sudden appearance in the doorway.

"Mike!" she called. "The Daisy Miller is closed—for the rest of the day. Clear them out. Every one of them. And you go with them. I do not want to be disturbed."

Ignoring the dismayed wailing of unhappy patrons, she slammed the door shut and turned the key in the lock. Then she rejoined Longarm, sitting once more on the sofa across from him.

"Could I have another drink, Longarm?" she asked. "Not so much this time, and I'll take it a bit slower. But it warms me, it does—just as your presence comforts me, as well. I thank you most sincerely for disposing of that worm. It is at times like this that I wish I had the strength of a man."

Longarm smiled as he poured another drink and handed it to her. "It is at times like this, Daisy, that I'm right glad I *do* have the strength of a man. Who *was* that son of a bitch, anyway?"

She took the drink from him and shook her head bitterly. "He was my first mistake on coming to Northfield. He's a widower. I am not married. We were both in business on the same street and neither was in competition with the other. We started seeing each other. Talk started." She shook her head bitterly. "And of course that's all it was—

97

talk. Bill could not get himself to ask a soiled dove to marry him."

"But of course that didn't stop him from continuing to see you. I know the type."

She sighed. "I suppose I can't blame him. It was one thing to be seen with a woman of my scarlet reputation. It even added frosting to his own, I suppose. He began to strut, as a matter of fact. But it was a horse of a different color to even consider the question of marriage. A few months ago I told him I did not want to see him anymore, not socially, that is. Well, he revealed his fangs then—and I realize what a lucky woman I am that this turd did not honor me with his name in marriage. Marriage to such a man would have been hell."

"It would—for you—have been impossible."

"Yes," she said. "It would have been just that. But now he insists on it. He demands that we marry. And that I see no one else. All of a sudden, it appears, he owns me."

"He could get dangerous," Longarm observed.

"Yes," she said, finishing her drink. "I have thought of that."

"You called him Bill. What's his full name?"

"Bill Wiggins."

Longarm smiled at that. "He was the reason I came into the saloon."

"You were looking for him?"

"Yes. There's a good chance he's mixed up in some shady dealings with a Matt Swenson."

Her face brightened in sudden awareness. "Of course," she said. "I can believe that, Longarm. Twice in the past month he has ridden out of town with Matt, and in each case it has set tongues wagging. On more than one occasion during the time I was seeing Bill, I found him and Matt deep in very secret business discussions—and always very late at night."

"Were there any late-night deliveries to his store, that you recall?"

"Yes," she replied promptly, almost eagerly. "There were. And usually it was soon after one of those secret meetings." She leaned close to Longarm, her eyes alight with mischief. "What is it, Longarm? What's that fool up to?"

Longarm laughed at Daisy's eagerness to know what it was that might soon cause Bill Wiggins to be indicted—or even better, hung. "Can't say for sure, Daisy. Things are getting a mite complicated. But there's just a chance Wiggins might be involved in some smuggling."

"Of course you realize the deputy is Bill's brother," Daisy pointed out.

"I noticed the resemblance a moment ago."

"And the sheriff is pretty thick with both men."

"The sheriff is pretty thick, period," he said, 'but I guessed as much."

She smiled brightly. "Well, then! It looks like this town has some more excitement coming to it, after all. It's about time these citizens got their chance to put up or shut up."

"How do you mean that?"

"All this town talks about is the time it stopped the James-Younger gang. To hear them tell it, every man jack of them was a roaring hero. Judging from the number of men they shot, there must have been two hundred bank robbers—and not a single one of them got away."

Longarm chuckled. "I'll be grateful for whatever assistance you can give me, Daisy. You've already helped some with what you've told me about Bill Wiggins. I've got quite a few leads—but at the moment I am like a cat who has one mouse in his teeth and sees three more runnin' across his path. I'm in danger of dropping the one to catch the others. I'm also waiting for a telegram I hope will tell me precisely why I was sent here. It may not be for the reason that was given to me—or to my chief in Denver."

"When do you expect it?" she asked.

"Tomorrow sometime."

She smiled and got to her feet. Reaching down, she took

99

his hands and pulled him to his feet. Then she pressed herself boldly against him and put her arms about his neck. She did not need to go up onto her tiptoes when she kissed him. After she had finished, she stepped back and smiled warmly at him.

"I can see what a gentleman you are, Longarm. You warm a lady's heart. You would not mind staying here with me while you wait for that telegram, would you?"

For answer, he lifted her easily in his arms and carried her from her office, through her sitting room, and on into her bedroom. He let her down gently on the bed. She did not lie back, however, but sat up and began to undress him, her fingers swiftly unbuttoning his vest, then his shirt, slipping them deftly back off his shoulders. She was only mildly surprised at the heft of his watch and fob as she neatly folded away the vest. When she began on the fly of his britches, Longarm busied himself with her dress, leaning over her to unhook it all the way down her back. They were both laughing softly and nuzzling each other by the time they finished their respective chores and found themselves naked in each other's arms.

He delighted in the long-limbed suppleness of her figure, allowing his hands to caress her completely. Soon she was on her back, pulling him gently onto her. Unwilling to see the beginning—and thus the end—of this come so swiftly, he held back, content to hold her close as he kissed her on the lips, deeply, hungrily. She groaned in ecstasy and tightened her arms about his neck. She moved her hips close under him and began to thrust upward hungrily. Longarm chuckled softly and pulled back to look down into her marvelous eyes.

"I'm glad you have enough sense to wait, Longarm," she panted, smiling back up at him. "But for my sake, don't wait much longer. It has been a long, long time since I have found myself under a real man."

He kissed her again, reaching down to feel of her warm moistness. Gently, he stroked her silky pubic mound. He

100

felt her opening under him, her legs splaying hungrily. Lunging with deft accuracy, she placed herself directly under him. As if he were abandoning himself to a bottomless pit, he allowed her hand to grasp his engorged member and guide it into her throbbing depths. The moment she had him, she uttered a tiny, delighted cry of triumph and wrapped her legs around his waist and locked them behind his back. Then, with a furious, shuddering grunt she pulled him in so deeply he could feel himself touching bottom.

Lifting momentarily from her, he saw her face lighten magically. She uttered a soft scream then, a breathless paean of delight, and pulling him back down, her hand on the back of his head guiding his lips to one of her nipples. His mouth encircling the swollen, stiffly erect nipple, he braced himself by resting his weight on his knees as he lifted her buttocks with his hands, squeezing their soft, firm muscles as he drove up into her with deep, regular thrusts.

Her body writhed under him, her gasps becoming short, sobbing bursts of pleasure. He felt the trembling begin deep within her. It spread, her muscles undulating until she was trembling from head to foot. Through it all, he devoured her breast, tugging at it with his tongue, smothering it with his lips. At last her head fell back, deep, sobbing gasps breaking from her taut throat as she let the joy of it take her completely. Lost in it, her entire body still trembling, she gave a final cry and went limp in his arms.

To his delight, Longarm found he was still rock-hard, still unsatisfied. He lifted his lips from her breast and kissed her on the mouth deeply, still holding her buttocks in his hands gently. Then, pulling back slightly, he said, "Can you feel me? I'm still ready."

"I know," she breathed. "I know."

She flung her arms more tightly about his neck. He felt the muscles of her vagina grow taut once again. "The other breast, Longarm," she cried. "Please."

He obeyed her at once and began thrusting fiercely. Her ankles still locked about his back, she pulled him into her

101

more deeply with each of his thrusts. This time, her trembling began sooner. But that was all right. Longarm was rapidly reaching a peak and he knew there was no way he was going to be able to hold back.

He suddenly let go of her buttocks and lunged deeper, pinning her to the bed, driving in so far he heard her shriek in a sudden, frightening cry of delight. Faster and faster he rocked, racing Daisy's quickening rush to her second orgasm—until he surpassed her and, with one mighty, triumphant thrust, slipped over the edge. He held himself deep within her, listening to her tiny cries of delight as she came. His shaking subsided and, spent almost completely, he rolled aside, leaving Daisy sprawled on her back beside him, one arm over her eyes, her mouth partly open, her tongue sliding back and forth across her upper lip. It was as if she had just eaten something indescribably delicious and was still savoring it.

"Just think, Longarm," she said. "We have the rest of the afternoon and all night."

Longarm laughed softly. "Please, leave enough in me so I can check on that telegram I'm expecting."

"All right," she said. "I'll leave that much."

As she spoke, she rolled gently onto him, her hand reaching down to check his condition. With a tiny cry of delight, she began nibbling on his ear. "You are some man, Longarm," she said. "So aptly named."

He stopped her talking with his lips. As he did so, for just a fleeting instant, he remembered the wild, almost insane light in Bill Wiggins' eyes as he broke in on them not so long before. To have lost as passionate and sensual a woman as Daisy could easily drive such a man mad with rage. Before he lost himself once again in the sweet madness of Daisy's lust for him, Longarm told himself he would be wise to keep a sharp eye out for Wiggins as long as he tarried in this town.

102

# Chapter 9

Longarm read the telegram, nodded in satisfaction, then read it a second time. "TREASURY CONFIRMS YOUR SUSPICIONS THEY ARE MISSING PLATES SENT TO NORTHFIELD BANK STOP FIND PLATES REPEAT FIND PLATES STOP VAIL U S MARSHAL DENV"

Folding the telegram and placing it in the side pocket of his frock coat, Longarm left the telegraph office and started down Division Street to the barbershop. It was late in the afternoon and the sunlight was very bright, he thought—until he realized it was just his own licentious habits of late that made him think that. He was reminded of the joke about the newlywed jasper who finally got up after a long while in the sack, lifted the windowshade to see what time of day or night it was—and went up with the shade. He turned into the barbershop, found an empty chair, and leaned back.

A bit later, his cheeks smooth and his longhorn moustache oiled and smelling as sweet as a whore on Saturday night, he pushed himself out of the chair, paid the barber, and left the barber shop. He paused a moment in the doorway to savor the clean air and the bright sunshine. Then, with a reluctant sigh, for he knew Daisy would protest his imminent departure from her bed and board, he continued on down the street toward the Daisy Miller.

103

He was crossing a narrow alley when a sudden movement to his right caught his eye. It was too sudden, too furtive. Even as he turned to see what it was, he was reaching for his Colt and dropping to a crouch. He glimpsed the muzzle of a shotgun poking out from behind an outside stairway and flung himself back out of the alley just as both barrels thundered. One charge tore away a portion of the building's corner as the other whistled harmlessly past Longarm into the street.

Ignoring the screams of passing women and the sudden thunder of men's bootheels on the wooden sidewalks behind him, Longarm launched himself back into the alley and was just in time to see the coattails of someone dashing from the other end of the alley and cutting down behind the buildings along Division Street. Longarm took after him at full tilt, grateful once again that he preferred low-heeled cavalry stovepipes. They were a damn sight easier to run in than those high-heeled riding boots most Western lawmen preferred. As he cut around the corner, his eyes searching for the running figure he had spotted earlier, he felt his right foot strike an unyielding obstruction—and went flying.

He came down hard on the rutted back alley and slid a ways on his shirtfront, his sixgun spinning away from him to slam finally against the side of an outhouse. There was no longer any running figure in front of him. He turned his head disgustedly to see what had tripped him and saw Tod Wiggins, his prominent front teeth highly visible as he grinned at Longarm and started toward him.

"Sorry about that, Marshal," he said. "I was coming to see what all the shooting was about, heard you coming, and ducked back just in time. Looks like my foot got in your way."

"So it did," Longarm said, just as a small army of townsmen who had charged down the alley after the running lawman crowded around Tod. "You probably didn't see anyone running from the alley just now."

"That's right." The deputy smiled. "I didn't."

104

Longarm retrieved his Colt and holstered it. "If you had, you would have tripped him up as neatly as you did me, I reckon."

"I don't know what you mean, Marshal." Tod turned then to face the eager townsmen, who were fairly salivating for details concerning the ruckus. "Looks like Deputy Long here is having some difficulty keeping on his feet lately. Might be he spends too much time in bed."

A roar of appreciative laughter greeted that remark. Every man there, it seemed, knew to which bed in particular Tod was referring. Longarm considered for a long moment the animated stick-figure who stood sniggering before him, then shrugged. There was no doubt in his mind that his and Tod's paths would cross again. Longarm would be looking forward to it.

Without comment, he strode past the deputy sheriff and pushed his way through the crowd. He was hoping Daisy's skills with a needle and thread would match her other considerable talents. His shirt was missing a button and there was a rip in the fabric just above his right vest pocket.

Pushing through the batwings of the Daisy Miller a moment later, his glance caught a very nervous barkeep and a few of the saloon's regulars up at the bar, with the town marshal in the midst of them, clinging to the bar for dear life. Longarm figured he'd heard about the attempted bushwhacking and was hoping no one would find him and demand action. Longarm decided not to bother him when he saw Bill Wiggins sitting at the green felt-topped poker table in the rear of the saloon.

Wiggins was not alone. A dark, surly-looking fellow dressed in a fussy vest, a velvet frock coat, and faun-colored britches—skin-tight, in keeping with the latest style—was sitting beside him. Both men watched him closely as he crossed the floor and approached their table.

The closer Longarm got, the more nervous Bill got. The fellow beside him, however, stiffened brazenly, then pushed his coat aside to reveal a gleaming, nickel-plated

105

and engraved, ivory-handled sixgun. It was almost too pretty a weapon to fire, Longarm mused to himself as he nodded and smiled coldly down at the overdressed dude.

"Where'd you get that iron, mister?" he drawled. "A Wild West show?"

The man's smile was as cold as Longarm's. "No," he said. "But you're close. From an idiot who had read too many Deadwood Dick stories."

"From the look of it, he had more money than sense."

"Now he has neither—and I have his weapon. Despite its flash, Marshal Long, it serves me well."

"I am afraid you have the advantage of me."

"Tyrone Wells, sir. My friends call me Ty."

"Well, Ty, if you had anything to do with that business down the street, I hope you know what you're doing. Pulling Bill Wiggins' dirty chestnuts out of the fire is liable to get you and that pretty iron in a heap of trouble."

"I—I had nothing to do with that!" Wiggins exploded fearfully. "I was here all the time! With Ty! Sitting right here. Ain't that right, Ty!"

Ty seemed slightly exasperated by his companion. He turned wearily to face him. "Not exactly, Bill. If you'll remember, you did step outside for a minute—to one of those small houses out back, if I'm not mistaken." He smiled up at Longarm. "As an alibi, it's not much, I admit, Marshal. But I am afraid my friend Bill doth protest too much. I do not remember you accusing him of anything."

Longarm smiled down at Bill then. "You know, he's right, Bill. Just what happened outside this saloon to make you so frantic for an alibi?"

"That shotgun blast! I heard it! Everyone in town knows by now that someone tried to bushwhack you."

"Everyone?"

Bill looked as if he were going to wet his pants. Beads of perspiration stood out suddenly on his forehead. He looked desperately in the direction of the barkeep, who looked swiftly away as he busied himself toweling down

106

the bar. "Yes," he said defiantly, "everyone."

"Was it you, Bill, that tried to bushwhack me?"

The man moistened dry lips. "Hell, no," he croaked. "I told you. I was here with Ty!"

"When you weren't outside in the alley, that is."

"Damn you, Ty!" cried Bill, turning on his companion. "Some help you are!"

Ty smiled thinly at Bill. "Smile, Bill, when you damn me—so I'll know you are just being friendly."

"Oh, hell, Ty. You know I was just . . ." Bill's voice trailed off in mute despair as he looked back up at the implacable face of Longarm, fear crowding his pale blue eyes.

"Killing me won't bring your girl back, Wiggins," Longarm told Bill coldly, his voice betraying now the contempt he felt for the man. "Seems to me you'd best stick closer to that business of yours—and while you're at it, you'd better see if you can't get along without stocking your shelves with any more of Matt Swenson's merchandise. A man like you just invites prosecution, if you get my drift."

Wiggins looked as if Longarm had just kicked him in the gut. His face didn't turn pale, it turned blue. He started to say something, to deny what Longarm was implying, but he didn't have the heart for it. "Come on, Ty," he said weakly. "This place has a stench to it."

As Wiggins pushed himself to his feet, Longarm took the front of his shirt with both hands, lifted him off the floor, turned about, and hurled him bodily toward the batwings. The man hit the floor running and stumbled awkwardly out through the batwings.

Tyrone Wells reached carefully down onto the chair beside him for his hat. As he stood up and squared the immaculate black Stetson carefully down onto his head, he addressed Longarm with a wry, almost apologetic smile. "I am sure you understand my position, Marshal. A man cannot always choose his employer. But he can—and must—serve him faithfully, despite that lamentable fact."

107

Longarm shrugged. "I didn't say a thing, Ty." Then he smiled wickedly. "But I'd say you got your work cut out for you this time."

Ty smiled back coldly. "I'll just have to keep him away from shotguns, Marshal."

"You do that, Ty."

Longarm watched Wiggins' dapper bodyguard—if that was indeed what he was—leave the saloon. Then he turned and walked over to the door leading to Daisy's office. He knocked softly, heard her voice bidding him enter, and pushed the door open.

Daisy was busy at her desk. At Longarm's entrance, she brightened considerably and put down her pen. Then she frowned.

"My God, Longarm! What happened to you? You're a mess."

"I was hoping you might be able to repair me."

She left her chair and hurried around the desk to him. "Of course, but what happened?"

He told her, briefly, about the attempt to murder him.

She was outraged. As she peeled off his vest and then his shirt, she said, "But here—in Northfield! It's so hard to believe. And you think it was Bill?"

"Or his brother."

"Of course. In some ways, Tod Wiggins frightens me more than Bill does. They are quite a pair. You'll have to watch them carefully, Longarm. But from now on, neither of those men will be served in the Daisy Miller. I'll tell Mike immediately."

"I wouldn't do that if I were you," Longarm suggested, as he sat down in the armchair and watched Daisy rummage in her desk drawer for a needle and thread. 'Let them come in if they want. You can find out more about your enemies if you let them talk. Besides, there's no sense in getting Bill any angrier with you than he is already. He's a mean, desperate man. His passion, his need for you, is turning him dangerous. There's really no telling what he'll do next."

108

"But he frightens me. I don't want him around me."

"Just tell Mike to watch him closely whenever he comes in here."

She sat down on the sofa across from him and began sewing. Her fingers moved swiftly, deftly, the needle flashing in the light, as she proceeded to mend his vest. She had taken the watch and the derringer out before she sat down and placed them gently on the table beside Longarm. "I guess that would be best," she said. "But I'm not worried." She flashed a smile at him. "Not while you're here."

"I'm leaving. Tomorrow, more than likely. My chief answered my telegram and it was what I suspected. Now all I have to do is bully our sheriff into helping me with a posse."

"Oh, Longarm. Tomorrow?"

"That's right."

She bent quickly to the vest, her fingers moving even more swiftly than before. In less than a minute, she bent and snapped the thread with a quick bite of her teeth. Then she put aside the vest and stood up.

"In that case Longarm, I want you to start saying goodbye. Right now."

He got up and took her in his arms.

"Carry me into the bedroom, she told him, "like you did the first time."

"Delighted," Longarm said, lifting her and carrying her from the room.

Sheriff Beazley was eating his supper in the hotel dining room. There were empty tables all around him, and as Longam approached the man, he realized this was because no one dared eat alongside the sheriff. There appeared to be a frightening possibility that an innocent diner might be caught by the sheriff's flailing arms and ground to death between the man's fearsome jaws.

Longarm pulled up a chair and sat down at the table across from Beazley. The lawman was so intent on his

109

business that he did not look up until he had disposed of a particularly large mouthful of mashed potatoes and gravy. He dabbed at his streaming chins with the corner of the huge bib he had tucked into his collar, then glanced up at Longarm.

Reaching for a mug of coffee, he said, "I didn't say you could join me for supper, Long."

"That's not why I'm here."

"If it's business, forget it. I'm off duty now. I'm eating."

"I noticed."

"Then why did you sit here?"

"I thought it might be a good idea to talk to you before you strangled yourself on a shinbone. I figure there's always a good chance you might not survive your next meal."

"Very funny," Beazley said, stabbing a huge slab of a steak with his fork. "If you have business, see me in my office tomorrow morning. Around ten."

He proceeded to slice through the steak. He cut himself a piece the size of a saucer and plugged his mouth with it. Somehow he got it all in. Then his eyes closed, the steak's red juices running out of the corners of his mouth, and began chewing—slowly, contentedly. The man seemed to be having a religious experience. Longarm had seen revivalists with that look on their faces whenever they dropped to their knees in communion with their Lord.

"All right, then. Ten o'clock tomorrow morning in your office," Longarm said, getting to his feet. "I'll expect you and the posse to be ready to ride out at that time."

Beazley almost choked. His face grew beet-red and he began to claw at his bib. Longarm strode swiftly around behind the sheriff and slapped him on the back. It was perhaps too enthusiastic a poke, since it drove the man violently forward, causing his face to slam into his platter. Spluttering like a beached flounder, Beazley hauled himself erect and attempted to turn around. Longarm pounded him one more time—just to make sure. This blow nearly knocked the man out of his chair. He was forced to grab hold of the table to prevent it.

110

"Damn you, Long!" Beazley cried, wiping off his face with his bib. "Keep your hands to yourself!"

"Sure. But I was afraid you were going to choke to death. And I didn't want that, Sheriff—not until you got that posse ready, anyway."

"Now see here. I told you before, I need authorization for such an undertaking! Where's your warrants? What fool's errand are we supposed to be on, anyway?"

"Recovering stolen federal property."

"Federal property? What federal property?"

"Federal currency plates that were stolen from the bank here in Northfield during that famed robbery by the James-Younger gang."

"Why, that's nonsense. It was *money* they stole. Nothing was said about federal plates."

"That's right. The Treasury didn't want it to be common knowledge that federal plates were floating around—not until the bogus bills began showing up, that is."

"I don't see how this changes anything. It's a federal matter. You've been sent here to handle it. Do so. And don't bother me about it. I have other concerns." He went back to his steak and potatoes.

"Then you won't mind if I bring in some federal deputies," Longarm said evenly.

Beazley looked up, a huge gob of mashed potatoes halted in midair just before his gaping mouth. "Federal deputies?"

"That's right. Bright fellows, all of them—and you can bet they'll be interested in Matt Swenson's smuggling and the cooperation he's been getting from the local merchants and the local law."

Beazley let his forkful of mashed potatoes return to his plate. "Now just a minute, Long. What are you implying?"

"Ain't implying a damn thing—saying it right out."

The man swallowed. Then he cleared his throat. "Five men, you said before. That's all you'll need?"

"I'd like more, but if that's all you can come up with, it'll have to do."

"I shall be a member of the posse myself," he said,

resignedly. "We are after a band of counterfeiters, is that it?"

"That's a start."

"And you have some idea where these miscreants may be found?"

"You've heard of Wolf Hollow, ain't you? The Tarnell gang?"

The man sucked in his breath and nodded. "Yes, Marshal, I have."

"Good. Then I'll join you and the posse tomorrow morning at ten in front of your office."

Beazley did not bother to reply. Longarm left him, and as he reached the door of the dining room he glanced back at the sheriff. Beazley was bent low over his plate, shoveling the food into his enormous mouth at a prodigious rate. It reminded Longarm of some unpleasant surgical procedure. He turned and left the place. He had been hungry when he entered the dining room a few minutes before, but now the thought of food made him sick to his stomach.

Longarm was not surprised at what he found waiting for him the next morning outside the sheriff's office. He was not surprised because Daisy had told him earlier that morning what Mike had overheard in the saloon.

In the posse already mounted up and waiting for him were Sheriff Beazley—aboard a big roan that was already beginning to wilt under the sheriff's cruel bulk—Bill and Tod Wiggins, and Ty Wells, looking as immaculate—and as cold—as a silver spoon. As Longarm guided his black carefully through the crowd of onlookers, he wondered who it was this posse was after—the Tarnell gang or the deputy U.S. marshal who had forced the sheriff to raise the posse in the first place.

112

# Chapter 10

Longarm had never ridden so far with four men with so little conversation, but he did not let it bother him. He was deep in his own thoughts as he rode, trying to unravel all the twine in this tangled ball of an assignment.

He kept thinking of that fellow with the ruined face, and poor, mad Anne—and Beverly, trying to take care of her sister in a shell of a town that was no more than a way station for robbers and cutthroats readying themselves for another assault on lawful society. And of course he had no confidence that this posse of his would have much luck against Tarnell's gang. For one thing, they'd be too busy trying to kill Longarm to fight Tarnell or his men. Still, Longarm had been in tighter spots in his life. He had learned to let polecats have their way for a while, since they usually managed to botch any concerted effort. More than likely it was their stink that made it impossible for them to stick together for long.

He was pretty certain, now, that the sheriff was in league with the Wiggins brothers and Matt Swenson. How that poor bank cashier, Welland, tied in with this business, Longarm could only guess. But if it was he that had brought the phoney bills to the attention of the Treasury, it could have been his way of double-crossing the sheriff and his men. By bringing in Longarm, he had, in effect, exposed all of them to the scrutiny of the law. It made a crazy kind of sense, especially since it was obvious that Welland had been no friend of Tarnell's gang. Indeed, the more Longarm thought on it, the more devilishly clever did such a move on Welland's part seem. He would have fingered the rival gang in addition to stopping Swenson's smuggling. The only thing that Longarm could not figure was his motive. Simple, cussed meanness did not seem to be enough motive to make a man go through such devious gyrations.

The hot sun had long since driven consecutive thought from Longarm's mind by the time the posse rode up to the Swenson farmhouse and dismounted. They all agreed with the near-dead sheriff that a rest was required, a rest and fresh drink, and perhaps some food. For a moment, as Longarm watched the corpulent sheriff slide wearily off his horse, he was worried the man was going to sink into the ground and dissolve into a massive puddle of fat. Tod Wiggins helped the man toward the house.

"Hello, the house!" Longarm cried.

As before, there was no response. By the time they reached the kitchen porch, he had called two more times with equal results. The posse entered the kitchen without further delay and slumped into chairs about the deal table. Longarm left them and walked into the bedroom.

It was no longer a shambles. Everything had been picked up and an earnest, if not very skillful, attempt had been made at cleaning up the floor. But all the sheets had been taken from the bed and the curtains from the window. The room was a sad echo of what Randy—out here in the middle of nowhere—had striven to make it. Her father must have been the one who cleaned up the room. As Longarm stood in the doorway, he had little difficulty in imagining the man's anguish as he went about the grim task.

Returning to the kitchen, he saw that Tod had managed to find some bread, and a pot of coffee was on, the wood stove already beginning to throw some heat. It was obvious that every one of the posse was more than familiar with the place.

"No sign of the girl, Marshal?" Beazley asked wearily, mopping his brow.

"None."

"Well, it is a pity. A very pretty girl, if a bit difficult. I wonder what happened to her. From your account of her room when last you passed this way, nothing good, I should imagine."

As they had ridden up to the farmhouse, Longarm had mentioned to the sheriff what he had found on his last ride past it on his way in to Northfield. The sheriff had expressed surprise and some concern. He had heard nothing about the matter, he assured Longarm.

"I'll bet Matt's fit to be tied," said Bill Wiggins, glancing nervously at Longarm as he spoke. Bill had, after all, been denying all along that he had had any dealings with the man.

Ty looked at Longarm. "You think this here gang of Tarnell's might have had something to do with it?"

Longarm took a deep breath. "That's what I'm afraid of, but I was figuring the two gangs kept their distance from each other."

Ty smiled at that. "Hell, Long. You know there ain't no honor among thieves—no matter what old Ned Buntline says."

"Yes, Ty," Longarm said, leaning his long frame against the doorjamb so that he faced all four of them. "I know that."

Ty chuckled as he accepted the hot coffee Tod placed beside him. "I had an idea you might."

They arrived in Pine Tree City late. Longarm had suggested they push on to the Badlands directly, sleeping under the stars. But even as he had made the suggestion, he knew there was no way in the world that these four men were going to let him escape the trap they were building for him in Pine Tree City.

The posse left their mounts at the livery stable, then the four men headed straight for the Cowboy's Palace. A sad-

115

dle-weary Beazley rocked unsteadily on his feet and had to be helped along by the Wiggins brothers. Longarm hung back to talk to the one-legged hostler.

"Here's something for your trouble, Hank," Longarm said, flipping a silver dollar at the man.

Hank shifted his crutch with amazing dexterity and snatched the spinning coin out of the air. His examination of the coin was swift and pleased. He glanced at Longarm. "You'll be wantin' somethin' for this, I'm thinking. Or are you just payin' off a bad conscience for waking me up a few days back in the middle of the night?"

"Right both times," Longarm told him. "Those four gents I just rode in with can't afford to ride out with me—if you get my drift. I'd appreciate it if you'd keep your eyes and ears open."

"Where you staying?"

"At the hotel with Beverly."

He squinted at Longarm. "You the one brought that crazy woman back to her?"

"Yes."

His wrinkled old face showed sudden concern as he shook his head. "Sad case, that. She must've met up with some bad ones."

"She did that. The Tarnell gang."

"Might've knowed. I'll keep alert," the man said. "Most gunslicks in this here town don't pay no more attention to a one-legged old codger like me than they do to a lamppost." He smiled wickedly. "You'd be surprised at what I can pick up."

"No, I wouldn't."

With a nod, Longarm left the livery and headed for Beverly's hotel.

Beverly was glad to see him, but as she closed the door behind him, Longarm could see clearly the terrible strain she was under. "How's Anne?" he asked her.

"Take off that dusty coat and hat, Longarm," she said, "and see for yourself."

116

A moment later, standing beside Beverly in her bedroom doorway, he saw why Beverly looked so troubled. Anne—freshly scrubbed and dressed in a lovely dress, her hair gleaming clean and combed out past her shoulders—sat like an oversized doll in a wooden, upholstered rocker. There was no expression on her face as she looked out the window that opened onto the grim back alleys of Pine Tree City.

"You see how it is, Longarm?" Beverly said, her voice soft, hushed. "Watch."

She entered the room and walked up beside Anne and suddenly snapped her fingers loudly less than an inch from Anne's ear. There was no response at all from the girl. Then Beverly passed her hand in front of Anne's eyes. Back and forth she passed it, but again there was no response, no sign at all that she had seen a thing—or that she even knew her sister was there. Beverly glanced over at Longarm.

"She might as well be blind as well as deaf," she said.

"Does she eat?"

"Yes. But I must feed her like a baby."

"She doesn't give you any trouble?"

"What do you mean?"

"No wildness. She was pretty hard for me to handle when we rode in from Wolf Hollow."

Beverly sighed and left Anne to walk past Longarm and into her sitting room. Longarm followed. "Do you know how much I have prayed for her to become wild again?" Beverly said. "To scream, perhaps. To try and claw me with her fingernails, even. Anything to show me that she can still feel, still react. As it is now, she's all but dead."

The big woman slumped wearily down into an upholstered chair, Longarm sitting across from her on the sofa.

"I don't know what to say, Beverly. But it's only been a week, less than that. Give her time."

"Of course. What choice do I have?"

Longarm nodded sympathetically, at a loss for words.

"She's my sister, Longarm. Perhaps this is my fault. If I had not left her in Connecticut all those years. If I hadn't become what I—"

117

Abruptly, her voice broke off. She bowed her face forward into her hands and began to weep like a bereaved little child. Longarm left the sofa and bent over her. Blindly, she reached up for him. He took her in his arms and let her sob. The storm, he could tell, had been a long time building.

At last, pulling away from him and dabbing at her swollen eyes with a lace handkerchief she produced from her bosom, she managed a dim smile and looked up at him. "Thank you, Longarm. I had to talk to someone. There's really no one here in this devil town for me to talk to. I swear, Longarm, this is simply no more than the last outpost before the gates of hell. And this is my home! My God, what a mess we make of our lives!"

"Your life ain't over yet, Beverly."

She looked at him for a long moment. "Isn't it? What do you see before you, Longarm, but a fat ex-madam, running a seedy hotel in the midst of nowhere? If my life is not over—and that of my sister—it is certainly giving a fine imitation of it."

"You're being too hard on yourself, Beverly. You are still a handsome woman, full of life."

"Is that what you see, Longarm? Truly?"

"Yes," Longarm replied deliberately, "that's what I see."

"Prove it."

"You mean . . .?"

"You know damn well what I mean. And you're man enough to be able to prove it, I'm thinking."

Longarm did not know what to say. But he did not want to hurt Beverly's feelings. Instinctively, he realized that he owed this to her, that without the kind of assurance she now wanted from him, she would not be able to deal much longer with the awful tragedy of her sister and of her life in Pine Tree City.

"First, I'll have the girl bring in a bathtub for you," she said, smiling through her tears. "You'll want to freshen up, I'm sure. And I'll put Anne to bed on her own cot in the other room."

118

"Yes," Longarm agreed, smiling suddenly. "That sounds like a good idea."

"And afterwards," beamed Beverly, "we'll have a grand meal brought in to us. How does that sound?"

"I told you, Beverly. You're still a handsome woman."

Longarm was astonished at the woman's vast, furnacelike warmth. As they embraced on her bed, he felt almost as if his eyebrows were being singed. He had been with ample women before, but Beverly was a revelation to him, nevertheless. She was not heavy at all, but light and supple—and her breasts were enough to satisfy any man. As he nuzzled her and pulled her closer to him, he reveled in the intoxicating overabundance of her.

"Mmmm," she murmured as he kissed, then toyed with her nipples. She hugged him gently closer until he felt as if she had surrounded him completely, shutting out all other sensations but the glow of her body. He felt himself growing at an alarming pace, rising eagerly, hungrily.

His eagerness surprised him. He was not usually so unwilling to hold back as this. But he was not going to argue with himself. He rolled her over and slid between her great thighs. She lifted her knees easily, spreading herself before him with an ease that amazed him. He swarmed up onto her and thrust home. She swallowed his erection effortlessly, then tightened her inner muscles about him with almost the strength of a fist. He laughed softly and began thrusting. She rocked back under him, lifting him. This woman needed no cushion under her buttocks.

Almost at once he felt himself reaching a climax. He tried to hold it back, but she grabbed him to her with such a fierceness that he knew there was no need to wait. She was with him, matching him thrust for thrust. A deep groan escaped her lips. He thought she was going to crush him as she hung onto him during her incredibly long, shuddering orgasm.

She did not relax, however, and though Longarm had

119

thought he was no longer in the running, he found that her skill was such that the muscles deep within her were already bringing him back.

They kissed passionately, and as she pulled her lips from his, she murmured in his ear, "You are right, Longarm. I am still alive. For the first time in a long, long while I know that I do still have hot blood in me. Do you feel it?"

"Yes," he said, laughing softly and nuzzling her breasts. "I certainly do, Beverly."

"Again!" she said. "And then again! I want to devour you, Longarm."

"You've already got the best part of me."

"He's growing so swiftly! Oh, my God, Longarm, he's so eager, so warm. I was right, wasn't I? You are the man to prove I am still alive."

But Longarm did not need to reply. He was caught up once again, and in a fury of thrusting he began to reach down once more for another climax. Rolling her head from side to side, Beverly lifted her knees and spread her legs wider. He felt himself driving still deeper within her. It was as if there were no bottom to her. Yet nothing was going to be allowed to prevent him from plumbing her depths.

And nothing did.

"What's that?" Beverly asked suddenly, sitting up in the bed and glancing through the bedroom doorway.

"It sounded like someone at the door." Longarm replied, sitting up beside her and reaching under his pillow for his .44.

"It's more a scratch than a knock," she said in puzzlement.

Slipping into a robe, Beverly left the bedroom to answer the door. Longarm swiftly flung himself into his pants, snatched up his Colt, and hurried out into the dim room after her. Beverly was approaching the door cautiously, looking back toward him. When she saw him emerge from the bedroom, she put her hand on the knob, waited for him to place himself behind the door, then pulled the door open.

The sound of a crutch striking the floor as Hank swung into the room caused Longarm to relax somewhat.

"It's Hank," Beverly said. She swung the door shut as soon as the old hostler was safely into the room.

With no place for Longarm to holster his Colt, he stood in the dimness of Beverly's apartment with it still in his fist. The old man eyed the weapon warily as he glanced at Longarm. "You told me to keep my eyes and ears open, mister."

"You can call me Longarm, Hank. We know each other by now."

"I'll light a lamp," said Beverly.

"No," Hank told Beverly quickly. "Don't do that. It'll give me away. They'll know you been warned."

"What is it, Hank?" Longarm asked. "What have you heard?"

"A couple of hardcases down on their luck have been hired to do you in, Longarm. They're on their way right now."

"Where are they coming from?"

"The Cowboy's Palace."

"All right. I'm obliged, Hank. I suggest you get out of here."

"Them's my thoughts, too."

"Here," Longarm said, fishing a coin from his pants' pocket.

"You already done paid me enough, Longarm. But watch out for them two. They're both mean enough to poison a rattlesnake."

He pivoted on his crutch then, to face the door. Beverly opened it for him and he swung out. Closing the door behind the hostler, she looked with alarm at Longarm.

"What are you going to do?"

"Go meet them. I don't want them coming here. You and Anne have been through enough already."

"Oh, Longarm! There's two of them!"

"I've been warned. That's given me the edge," Longarm said, hurrying into the bedroom for the rest of his clothes.

121

# Chapter 11

When Longarm stepped out into the street, he noted that the Cowboy's Palace was the only saloon open on the corner. He had taken no more than a few steps along the sagging boardwalk before the lights inside the place began to fade as, one by one, its lamps were extinguished.

Longarm wondered how much it had cost the sheriff for that bit of help, and then realized that he was probably giving the man too much credit. It was pretty late, and the place had to close sometime. Still, he realized, it would not be a bad idea to hold up a minute and get his eyes accustomed to the darkened street. Anyone skulking along the boardwalk toward the hotel, of course, would be suspect.

He pulled into the shadow of a boarded-up storefront, his hand resting on the butt of his Colt, and went perfectly still. After a few moments his eyes became sharp enough for him to be able to pick out someone moving toward the hotel from the other side of the street, coming from the direction of the now-dark saloon. He caught only fleeting glimpses of the moving shadow as it passed from darkness into dimness. The man was crouched low, Longarm noticed, and was holding something in his hand, a rifle possibly. Longarm drew his big Colt.

And then Longarm heard the sound of quick steps on the boardwalk, approaching him on this side of the street and

123

coming from the same direction. Hank had said there were two of them. Longarm braced himself to move in behind the man as soon as he passed him. Abruptly, the footsteps ceased. The tall deputy strained forward to listen and thought he heard footsteps running along the ground, growing fainter with each second.

In the alley that led behind the hotel, the second gunslick was figuring to get at Longarm by breaking into the rear of the hotel. Cursing softly, Longarm ducked from the doorway and darted for the alley entrance. As he reached the alley and dropped into it, he thought he heard the fellow on the other side of the street leaving the boardwalk to overtake him, his bootheels pounding in the dust.

Which meant that Longarm was now between his two would-be assassins.

Longarm had almost reached the end of the alley when a gunshot lanced the night ahead of him. He heard the bullet slam into the wood siding behind him, and ducked low, returning the fire instantly with his Colt. But there was no second shot, and he kept going. As soon as he reached the end of the alley, he turned the corner and flung himself along the gound holding his Colt out in front of him.

A second shot exploded from halfway up a wooden stairway to his right, the slug slamming into the ground inches from where his left hand was supporting him. Fragments of dirt leaped up to dig at his eyes and face. He rolled over swiftly and kept rolling, then scrabbled for cover behind an outhouse. Even as he flung himself behind it, another shot bit a chunk of weathered board from the corner of the small structure.

Longarm went around to the other side of the outhouse, crouched low behind the noisome building, and waited— as silent as death, his mouth slightly open so his panting would not be heard. It felt as if he had waited for another century to begin—though it could not have been more than a couple of minutes—before he heard the sound of someone making his way cautiously down the flight of stairs. Longarm kept himself motionless until the jasper reached the floor of the alley. Then he straightened up and flattened himself against the wall and edged himself all the way around the outhouse until he was facing the alley. He peeked around the edge of the privy and saw a man moving in a crouch from the stairs to the other side of the outhouse, his sixgun extended in his right hand.

The dim moonlight filtering into the alley gave Longarm only a shadowy picture of the man. He appeared to be no more than five-feet-five or thereabouts, and wore a hat with the brim turned down on all sides of the crown. The muted jingle of his spurs was the only sound he made as, still crouching, he disappeared behind the far side of the outhouse. Swiftly, Longarm moved out into the alley, darted around, and came up behind the fellow before he could make the next corner.

"Drop your weapon, friend," Longarm told the jasper, his voice edgy.

"Oh, shee-it," the man said. He sounded like someone just up from the South.

"Drop it, I said."

But the man was game. He lunged to one side, spinning about as he did so, his iron up and belching fire. But Longarm had expected the move and had already ducked back behind the corner of the building, his double-action Colt jumping in his hand, thundering twice in rapid succession.

The little man's round bit away a chunk of the building over Longarm's head, but Longarm's two shots found their mark, catching the gunman belt-high. The force of the two .44-40 slugs sent the man slamming awkwardly back. His pistol still in his hand, he tripped over a low back porch and went spinning to the ground. He came down on his stomach and began to twist slowly. In the darkness, it looked as if he were trying to crawl into himself.

Longarm's first instinct was to drop beside the wounded man to see what he might do to alleviate his suffering, but a warning sounded deep within him, and he flung himself

125

around to head for the stairway. The second man was in this alley somewhere, and those shots would bring him before they brought any help—if any help was conceivable in this place.

But already moving into the shadows under the stairs was the second man, a rifle—no, it was a double-barreled shotgun—in his hand. "You son of a bitch," the second gunslick snarled at Longarm. "You done killed Toby!"

"It was him or me," Longarm said calmly, his eyes riveted on the twin bores that peered unblinkingly across the alley at him.

"Well, now you're gonna get yours, lawman, and it'll be a pleasure."

Longarm was still holding his weapon. He had no intention of taking both of those barrels without giving something back in turn. He flung himself to his left and brought up his Colt and fired—a split second before the other fellow let both barrels loose.

It sounded as if a Civil War cannon had gone off, and Longarm felt a few pellets of buckshot pluck at his left sleeve. He struck the uneven ground heavily and tried to bring his gun up to fire a second time at his assailant, who was still standing, untouched, in the shadow of the stairway. The man had dropped the empty shotgun and was already bringing up his sixgun. It blazed in his hand. The round slammed into the ground just in front of Longarm. Dirt exploded in his face, blinding him.

Longarm heard another shot, from farther away, it seemed—and waited for the round to punch into his prostrate body. But he felt nothing. He heard the man under the stairway groan. Then came the sound of a sixgun being dropped. Digging the dirt out of his eyes, Longarm glanced up to see his assailant sagging slowly to the ground.

Help had come! But who the hell . . .?

Glancing down the alley, Longarm thought he glimpsed a running figure. It was only an instant before it vanished down an alley out of sight. Yet, in that single glance,

126

Longarm thought he had caught sight of a sixgun gleaming brightly in the shadowy figure's hand.

It took only a moment for Longarm to see that nothing could be done for the two men. The one Longarm had shot was dead, the other close to it. He holstered his Colt, brushed himself off, and started back down the alley. When he reached the street, the darkness seemed to swell suddenly as men left the doorways and the shelter of porches to swarm toward him—like a silent tide of cockroaches coming out of the woodwork.

They were surprised to see him—but none seemed expecially pleased that he had managed to escape his two assailants. They stopped about ten feet from him to stare silently, bitterly, at this minion of the law who had survived one of their kind. There was not a man in the town, Longarm realized, who had not known beforehand that two men had left the Cowboy's Palace to claim the price on the federal lawman's head.

Doc Gurney broke through the sullen ring of gunslicks and halted before Longarm. "You look all right," he said, weaving slightly. "What about them other two?"

"How'd you know there were two of them, Doc?"

"That was the talk, Longarm."

"One of them's already dead. You might be able to help the other."

The doctor nodded, then weaved groggily past Longarm into the alley. As he did so, Sheriff Beazley and Tod Wiggins pushed their way through the crowd. A sick smile was pasted on the rotund sheriff's face.

"Heard the shooting, Long. Must be some old acquaintances of yours trying to even the score. We lawmen don't make many friends over the years. Glad to see you're all right."

Longarm resented having Sheriff Beazley count himself a lawman in the same league as himself, but he said nothing as Tod Wiggins and Ty Wells joined the sheriff. They took a position beside the man and nodded warily at Longarm.

127

Bill Wiggins' face seemed dark with frustration. It was obvious he had not hoped to see Longarm emerge alive from that alley. Hank had not said who had hired those two men, but Longarm was willing to believe it was Bill Wiggins, with his brother and the sheriff as the main driving force.

But Ty Wells' role in all this was not clear to Longarm. He was sure, now, that it was Ty he had just seen running from the alley. Yet how could Longarm be certain that Wells had meant to save Longarm's life with that shot? In the darkness of that alley, Ty could easily have mistaken the assailant for Longarm.

Longarm looked around at the encircling men. "If any one of you is itchin' to take up where those two back there left off, step forward," Longarm told them. "Don't be shy. Sheriff Beazley here will be glad to stand right behind you— out of the line of fire."

The sheriff pulled himself up indignantly. "Marshal Long, that's a dastardly inference."

"Not only that," said Ty, smiling sardonically at the sheriff, "but it is also true."

The sullen crowd broke then, and in a moment the men had sifted back into the darkness of the town. Longarm watched them go for a moment, then nodded a grim good-night to the sheriff and the rest of his posse, and strode back to the hotel.

Early the next morning, Anne joined Beverly and Longarm at the breakfast table. Longarm was humbled at Beverly's patience as she fed the silent, unresisting Anne. Anne ate a good breakfast, Longarm noted, but each morsel of it had to be shoved into a slack, uncooperative mouth. At times it was messy, but Beverly uttered not one word of reprimand. Longarm found himself relieved somewhat when Beverly led Anne back to her chair in the bedroom.

As Beverly sat back down to have her final cup of coffee with Longarm, he asked her, as gently as he could, what,

128

if anything, Beverly might have found out about her still-missing father—the object of Anne's fruitless quest.

"Nothing. I have given up, Longarm. Though, God knows, I could sure use the man's help if he's still out there somewhere."

"You said the last you heard he was in this place."

"That's right."

"Not the best place in the world for an honest man trying to make his way in the world."

"I realize that, Longarm. But, as I told you, when I got here there was no sign of him."

"What's his name, Beverly? And yours too, for that matter."

"You know a woman like me never likes to be known by her true name, Longarm. It's an unwritten law. When we lose our honor, we lose our name as well—our good name, that is."

"You can tell me, Beverly."

She sighed. "Of course. I know I can. I know how different you are from the apes I am used to dealing with."

"Thank you, Beverly. And thank you for giving it away free last night—something you said once was not quite your style."

"I've said a lot of things in my life I'd like to take back. Thank you for last night, Longarm. It was my pleasure. Thank you for what you gave me."

"So what was your good name—and that of your father?"

"Fredricks. My father's name was Calvin."

Longarm had been in the act of picking up his coffee. He almost dropped the cup.

"What's wrong, Longarm?" Beverly asked, alarmed.

Slowly, carefully, Longarm put down the cup. "I ain't just sure, Beverly. Not quite, that is. But you did mention that your father was an engraver, didn't you?"

"Yes, one of the best, as I understand it."

Longarm took out his wallet, opened it, and took from it a small piece of paper. It was the list he had found on

129

Welland's dead body, containing the numbers on the missing federal plates. But as he unfolded the paper, it was not the banknote numbers his eyes searched for—but the initials "C. F." and the cryptic comment, "The Best."

He passed the slip across the table to Beverly. "One of the men in Tarnell's gang, a strange jasper with a terrible acid burn on his face, was called Cal by the gang members. I suspicion he may be a counterfeiter employed by the gang."

"But you don't think that man—and my father—are the same? There must be many men out there—in this town, even—named Calvin."

"Yes, of course," Longarm said, patting her hand to comfort her, and gently taking the piece of paper back.

Beverly frowned. "A counterfeiter, you said?"

"That's right."

"And father was an engraver."

"Yes."

"Oh, my God. It couldn't be. It is just a coincidence."

"I hope so," Longarm told her sincerely.

"That man with the scarred face . . . he was one of those who . . ." She could not bear to give her thoughts the tangibility of words, lest she give them a reality she could not face.

Again Longarm reached over to rest his hand on hers. "Like you said, Beverly. It could be just a coincidence."

She nodded, her expression preoccupied as she attempted to recall something. Then she looked at him, her eyes filled with sudden pain. "You remember I said I had the feeling that I was . . . being protected, Longarm?"

"Yes, I remember."

"Wouldn't that explain it? If this man . . . was my father, and if he knew I was here, wouldn't he make it his business to see that Tarnell and his gang spread the word to leave me be?"

"I reckon that might follow."

"Oh, Longarm," she said, her voice hushed with the horror of it. "I feel sick."

130

"Remember what you said just now, Beverly? There are many Calvins out there. This could be just a coincidence."

"But those initials—"C. F." Those are my father's initials."

"Calvin Fredricks."

"Yes."

"Let me find out for sure, Beverly. Wolf Hollow is my next stop—if I can survive my posse, that is."

The blonde girl entered then, to clear off their table. Beverly, her face showing the strain she was under, left Longarm and went in to her sister. Longarm put his hat on, checked his weapons, then paused a moment in the bedroom doorway to bid Beverly goodbye and thank her for her hospitality.

There were tears in the woman's eyes as she turned from gazing at her sister. "Good luck, Longarm," she managed. "Be careful of those apes in that damned posse of yours."

"I will," he told her.

# Chapter 12

Sheriff Beazley, puffing as he roweled his horse alongside Longarm's black, cleared his throat portentously. Longarm glanced at the sheriff. Perspiration was pouring down his face and he was making every effort to stand in his stirrups rather than let his blistered ass rest upon the saddle.

"Your remark last night was not kind, Marshal," the sheriff protested. "Not kind at all. As a matter of fact, I got a good look at both corpses this morning and recognized each one as a wanted man. Their dodgers are resting on my desk in Northfield. What must have happened was they heard you were in town and concluded they had better get you before you got them. It's as simple as that."

"Why, thank you, Sheriff. That makes me feel a whole lot better. Yessir, a whole hell of a lot better. Tell me, who do you suppose let on I was in the vicinity?"

The man blanched, then tried to say something, but thought better of it, and pulled his horse back, leaving Longarm to ride on alone as before.

They were within sight of the Badlands not long after, and by nightfall they were riding up the narrow stream that led into the dark hills, Longarm still leading the way. Hearing someone riding up behind him, Longarm turned about in his saddle. It was Ty Wells. The man had kept to himself since leaving Pine Tree City. Despite the repeated pleas of Beazley, Longarm had allowed only one brief rest at noon to water the horses; and during that respite, Longarm had not failed to notice that the dapper Wells had kept to himself, saying not a word to any of his companions, except on one occasion when he had been especially short with Bill Wiggins.

Longarm nodded cordially to the man as he pulled his horse up alongside Longarm's black.

"Notice anything, Marshal?"

Longarm frowned and then looked back along the trail. It was a narrow one and wound close to the base of a cliff. On the other side of the trail there was a precipitous drop to the roaring stream far below. Longarm kept watching. After a while, he turned back and smiled at Ty Wells.

"We've lost some of our posse."

"Ordinarily, I'd say good riddance, Marshal. But not in this case."

"No," Longarm agreed. "Not in this case."

"I suppose you know what's up."

"Unfinished business."

"Precisely. That business they botched last night."

"Thanks to you."

"I was wondering if you saw me."

"Couldn't be sure in that light. Or that you hit the man you were aiming at."

"I was hired by a very frightened Bill Wiggins to protect him from a man who had beaten him fearfully and then thrown him bodily from the apartment of his fiance. That was how you were presented by Wiggins. It didn't take me long, however, to realize that I was being paid to protect the wrong man."

"I ain't in the market for a bodyguard, Ty."

He grinned. "I know that. But since we started out this morning, I'm unemployed. You might say I'm just along for the ride—and anything else that offers itself."

"Those three are trying to cover dirty tracks, and they

will make trouble. They ain't careful men—and they can be dangerous."

"Exactly my assessment. Sometimes it is such jackasses that get all the rest of us into hellfire and brimstone."

Longarm turned about in his saddle once again. "You saw what direction they rode off in?"

Ty Wells pointed to the rim of the canyon, cutting the sky above them. "I overheard them. They figure to ride along the rim until they find a spot to bushwhack you."

"And you, as well."

Ty Wells shrugged. "Like I say, if that's what offers itself."

"What do you say we do what we can to even the odds a mite?"

"Suits me."

Longarm rode a ways farther until he came to a narrow game trail that wound its way upward, apparently to the rim. Dismounting, he and Wells led their horses up the trail. It was not easy. The horses had trouble with the loose footing caused by the talus that littered the slope. Just before they reached the canyon's rim, it looked for a moment as if Wells were going to lose his bay. It took both Wells and Longarm to pull the animal the final ten yards or so onto the rim.

Longarm found tracks to follow soon after. The two men mounted up and followed the three desperadoes along the rim for close to a mile. Longarm enjoyed Ty's company. The man said little, and everything he said had value. He did not seem to miss anything, and he was a fine horseman. His surly manner, Longarm soon discovered, was no indication of the true man underneath, but a mask he presented to the world—a "keep off" sign that warned others not to get too close. And this desire to stay clear of others was born of a bone-deep awareness of how feckless and treacherous his fellow men could be, as Longarm discovered after a few brief exchanges with Wells concerning the sheriff and the Wiggins brothers. The man was a damn fool romantic,

135

after all. He was looking for an honest man—and even more foolish, for a faithful woman. As a result, Longarm was convinced that Ty Wells would be forever and continually disappointed.

It was Ty who first spotted the horses tethered in a narrow cut near the rim.

"We better get off these animals," Longarm commented, pulling up.

Ty nodded and dismounted. The two men found a birch grove, tied their horses to saplings well within the trees, then pulled their rifles from their saddle scabbards and headed back toward the rim. A quarter of a mile farther on, Longarm spotted the sheriff sitting on a flat rock, mopping his brow.

How in hell, Longarm wondered as he and Ty crept up behind the man, did such a barrel of lard get to be sheriff? It was a question he soon forgot as a rifle shot from above and behind them sent a slug whistling past his moustache. As he and Ty flung themselves to the ground, they found themselves caught in a wicked crossfire from two rocky prominences on both sides of the perspiring sheriff. As luck would have it, the emplacements Tod and Bill Wiggins were using were so situated that they not only gave a clear view of the canyon trail below, but of the rocky ground over which Longarm and Ty had been advancing.

With a scream of terror, the sheriff flung himself to the ground behind the rock upon which he had been sitting, disappearing from sight with a suddenness that was almost comical.

"Marshal!" he cried from behind the rock. "This was not my idea! Those two brothers! They've got it in for you. Believe me, I've had no part in their treacherous schemes!"

"Shut up and keep your ass down," Longarm advised, chuckling despite the angry bullets singing around him.

As a matter of fact, the sheriff's sudden panic was the only thing about their current dilemma that gave Longarm any comfort.

Crouched beside him, Ty swore softly. He was trying

136

to use rocks lower than his ass for cover. Longarm was trying to do the same. The rounds from the two rifles were buzzing close over their heads, occasionally ripping up the ground in front of them and whining off the rocks. It was only a matter of time before a round found one of them.

Longarm was in the act of pulling his rifle around to get the bead on one of the Wigginses, when he heard rifle fire from behind the rocks where the two brothers were holed up. At once, he heard a cry of pain and then saw the figure of Tod Wiggins tumbling down a narrow path to the rock-strewn flat below. The plight of his brother caused Bill Wiggins to show himself.

Longarm's rifle had been trained on that section of the rocks. Swiftly, Longarm sighted and fired. Rock shards exploded in front of Bill. The man cried out, dropped his rifle, and disappeared back into the rocks.

"Let's go," said Ty, scrambling to his feet. "We got help!"

As the two men raced to the side of the fallen deputy, Longarm saw Matt Swenson appear from the rocks above them, his Winchester trained on them. From that distance and that vantage point he could not miss.

Longarm and Ty held up.

"Some help we got," said Longarm.

"Hold it right there, Longarm," Matt Swenson called out. "I won't hurt you none if you'll give me a hearing."

"That'll be a change."

"I know what you think, and I don't blame you. But I think we two should put the past behind us."

"If that means you won't blow our heads off, mister," said Ty, "then I'm all for it."

Swenson grinned coldly. "I see you've got a sensible head on your shoulders, dude."

"That he has," Longarm seconded. "Now what do you want?"

"To join forces."

"You need men?"

"I've disbanded that gang, Longarm. One of them pretty

137

near died from that bullet you sent into him, and the rest think my present business is too dangerous."

"And what might that be?"

"I think my daughter has been taken by Tarnell and his boys. I think she's a prisoner in Wolf Hollow. I'm going in after her. I would appreciate your help."

"You're sure she's there?"

"Yes, damn it. It's the only place she could be. I've made inquiries. Seems they already had someone to keep them company until you took her. They remembered Randy had helped you some, so they took her. As a punishment to both of us, I guess. Randy told me about you, Longarm—how you'd handled Tarnell's boys. And how much she liked you."

"Put down that rifle," Longarm said. "You don't need it. Not for now, anyway."

Matt nodded, rested the rifle in the crook of his arm, and started to climb down from the rocks. As he was doing this, Longarm and Ty inspected Tod Wiggins. The man was dead, a thumb-sized opening in one temple, a hole the size of a fist on the other side of his shattered skull.

The sudden thunder of horses' hooves pounding along the rim erupted behind them. They spun as the sound faded.

Longarm said, "Looks like the sheriff and Wiggins are on their way back to Northfield."

"Where they will pray the Tarnell gang finishes us," said Ty.

Longarm flashed a smile in the darkness. "I'm purely going to hate to disappoint them."

Matt Swenson gained the flat and approached them. Longarm was familiar with the man's appearance from the time when he had watched him enter the Cowboy's Palace and on another, more painful occasion when the man had calmly sat his horse, aimed, and attempted to put a bullet through Longarm's head. He looked older now, however—as if he had aged suddenly. Of course, Longarm knew the reason for that.

Swenson's rugged, craggy features seemed to have been

138

softened, blunted, as if by a blow. His eyes were haunted, but burning with a fixed, almost demoniac intensity. His blond hair which had reminded Longarm at once of Swenson's daughter, was streaked with gray now, those locks of it that hung below his tan, flat-crowned Stetson. He wore a dusty, fringed buckskin shirt, Levi's, and riding boots, the same uniform he had worn on the day he and his men had held up those teamsters.

As Swenson pulled up in front of them, Longarm said, "One question, if you don't mind."

"What is it?" the man asked wearily, his tall, craggy figure still impressive.

"Beazley and the Wiggins brothers have been in cahoots with you for some time now. Am I right?"

The man shrugged. "I won't argue that. But I deal with other merchants in other towns."

"The point I'm making," Longarm said, "is this. If you know those men, why in hell didn't you get them to help you, instead of us?"

Swenson snorted bitterly. "Sure as hell you must know the answer to that, Longarm. Those men aren't worth a pitcher of warm spit. I figure you and this dude with you are what I need to save Randy. I need guns I can count on. If they've got my daughter in there, Longarm, you know what that means. I heard about that crazy woman you took back from them. I don't want that to happen to Randy."

"I don't either, Matt," Longarm said. He looked down then at the body of Tod Wiggins. His brother had left him like this and ridden off with the sheriff. So much for brotherly love. "What are we going to do with this one?"

"Leave him to the buzzards," Matt said. "He won't be much of a meal for them, but it's his turn now, anyway. Tod's left his share for them birds in his time."

"All right, then," said Longarm, "let's move out."

For close to an hour the three men crouched on a ledge overlooking Wolf Hollow, waiting for darkness to settle over the buildings below. While they waited, Matt con-

139

firmed Longarm's suspicions concerning Tarnell. Each outlaw on the dodge who took refuge in his hideaway had to exchange his hard currency for federal notes supplied by Tarnell. The only thing was, the federal notes were counterfeit, something the hapless outlaw paying for Tarnell's aid would not know. It was a surprise to Matt, also. The outlaws that came to Tarnell exchanged their hard-won booty for bogus money.

Ty grinned. "Like I said, Longarm, there's no honor among thieves."

Matt muttered something and peered anxiously down at the ranch. "Damn it," he said. "This moon is getting brighter. I don't want to wait any longer."

Longarm nodded. "All right. Let's do it this way. Split up. I'll take the cabin, 'cause I know how it's laid out. You two see what you can do about a diversion, something to attract their attention if I need to go in after Randy."

"What kind of a diversion?" asked Matt.

"How about stampeding their horses?" suggested Ty.

"That ought to do it," Longarm agreed.

"Right," said Matt. "That's what we'll do. Come on, dude. Let's go."

Without a word, Ty left with Matt Swenson. Longarm waited until they had both disappeared into the darkness before he made his way down the slope to the hollow. He came out close to the building across from the cabin where he had imprisoned Buck, and in which he had spotted the printing press. Longarm knew that if he searched the other rooms in that building, he would likely find those federal plates.

But it was Randy they wanted now—not the plates. If Randy was not here—and that would be good news indeed—then Longarm would come back for those plates.

Keeping to the shadows, Longarm moved swiftly across the compound. When he reached the cabin, he darted around to the rear of it and peered into the same room where he had found Anne. The room was dark and appeared to be

140

empty. He moved on to the next window and peered in. All during their wait on the ledge above, the sound of the men's revels had been coming to them clearly. Now Longarm was able to see their condition firsthand. A few were playing poker, but most were just standing around, drinking. He could not see Randy, however.

And then a group of men moved closer to the poker table to take part in an argument, and Longarm saw Randy. She was sitting in a corner, fully clothed, her knees drawn up to her chin, her arms wrapped tightly about her knees. There were bruises on her face and her lips were swollen, but outside of that she did not look too bad. No matter what these men had done to her, they had not destroyed her spirit.

Longarm moved back to the other window. It was still open. Tarnell had learned nothing from Longarm's last visit, it seemed. Longarm pulled himself up over the windowsill, then moved silently across the room to the door. Carefully, he pulled it open a crack and peered into the room. From this vantage point, he could see Randy more clearly. She was wide awake, he saw, and was obviously very anxious to be somewhere else. He could imagine what she must already have suffered at the hands of these animals.

Where the hell was that diversion? Longarm wondered irritably.

Then Longarm saw Finn Tucker leave a group and walk over to Randy. He knelt by her and said something to her. Randy's hand snaked out and slapped Finn so hard that his head snapped around from the force of the blow. The men behind laughed at his discomfiture. Finn laughed also, then punched Randy so hard it knocked her head back against the wall. Longarm had all he could do to hold himself back.

He heard a sound behind him and spun about to see a dark figure sitting up on the bed. The man had been sleeping so quietly that, in the darkness, Longarm had not even noticed him. Now, with the bright stripe of light illuminating the room, he saw that it was the same man he had seen riding into Pine Tree City with Tarnell on the day

141

they took Brad Tarnell's body in for burial. With a quick stride, Longarm reached the side of the bed and slammed the man brutally on the side of his face with his Colt. The sound of the bone-crunching blow filled the little room, and its force sent the man tumbling headlong off the bed. Longarm moved swiftly back to the door. But no one had noticed. The noise level in the big room had been enough to drown out the sound.

Randy's head was bent forward and he saw a tear sliding down one cheek. Damnit! Longarm thought bitterly. What was keeping those two?

Two shots exploded in the night outside the canyon. Almost immediately, there came the sound of horses whinnying, followed by the tattoo of hooves as the horses raced past the cabin. At once the men broke for the door. But as they swarmed out through it, guns drawn, gunfire from outside caught one of them and spilled him back into the cabin. Others still managed to crowd out the door, however.

Longarm darted from the bedroom and reached down for Randy. The men were so busy at the side door—some shooting out into the darkness, others crowding out through the doorway—that Longarm was able to pull the startled Randy to her feet without anyone seeing him. Randy was still a little groggy from that blow Finn Tucker had given her, so Longarm had to help her into the bedroom. He was assisting her through the window when her gasp alerted him. He spun about and saw a dark figure standing in the bedroom doorway. He fired at the man and sent him reeling back into the other room. Alerted now to his presence, those men remaining in the room started firing at him. Longarm sent two more shots at the crowd of men, then flung himself out through the window after Randy.

He grabbed her arm and pulled her along toward a grove of trees across an open space, hoping that in the darkness they might be able to find adequate cover. But as they ran, two of Tarnell's gang appeared from around the corner of the cabin and ran over to cut them off. Longarm saw the

142

glint of their sixguns in the bright moonlight. He pushed Randy to the ground to keep her out of the line of fire, and then got off two quick shots at the approaching outlaws. His first shot went wild; his second caught the nearest one. Then the hammer of his Colt clicked futilely on an empty chamber.

The second outlaw laughed and swung up his sixgun. Longarm fumbled at his vest, but was pretty certain he was not going to be able to get his derringer in time. With a cry of dismay, Randy jumped to her feet and flung herself between Longarm and the outlaw just as the man fired. Longarm felt Randy's body shudder as the slug slammed into her. The outlaw, still grinning, strode closer, but by that time Longarm had his derringer ready. He brought it up and fired both barrels into the man's face. It was as if the darkness around them had swallowed up the man's features as he cried out and spun to the ground.

But Longarm was not worried about him as he gently lowered Randy's body to the ground. In the moonlight, he saw her eyes flicker open. Her arms tightened around his neck.

"You came for me, Longarm!" she whispered.

"Yes," he replied. "And your father, too."

"Where is he?"

"Right here," said Matt.

Longarm looked up. Matt Swenson was standing behind him, looking down at his fallen daughter, a stricken look on his face.

"She took a bullet meant for me," Longarm told the man bitterly. "I couldn't stop her. It happened too fast."

"Let me be alone with her," Matt said, without looking at Longarm.

Longarm got up and stepped back, dimly aware of Ty approaching from the direction of the cabin. He saw Randy's father kneel by her and then take one of her hands in his. In the bright moonlight, Randy's golden hair seemed to glow eerily—while her face had a shiny, deathly cast to

143

it. And then Longarm heard a sob break from Matt Swenson's throat and saw him bend his head suddenly over his lifeless daughter.

Longarm cursed miserably. They had saved Randy from these animals—but they had lost her all the same.

# Chapter 13

Ty was holding his shoulder. His face was white and drawn, but there was a cocky light in his eyes. As Longarm drew the man away from Matt Swenson and the dead Randy, anxious to give the old bandit time to shed his tears, he asked Ty how badly he had been hurt.

"Just a scratch," Wells replied. "Took away some fat and ruined a fine shirt. Maybe that lady of yours will sew it for me."

"She's good at that," Longarm said, glancing back at Matt Swenson. "Maybe she will."

"What happened here? How badly is the girl hurt?"

"She's dead, Ty. She took a slug for me."

The man swore softly and, with his good hand, took off his hat. He moved past Longarm and approached the dead girl, halting at a discreet distance. Longarm took a deep breath and glanced swiftly around him. It seemed uncannily quiet after all that hell. And then he began counting mentally the men that had fallen before his guns. Abruptly, the silence was shattered by the quick thunder of galloping horses. Turning swiftly, Longarm heard the slap of leather and the faint chink of bits as two—possibly three—horses were ridden hard out of the hollow.

"Goddamnit," he said softly. "Some of them are getting away!"

145

He began to run back toward the cabin. As he did so, he glimpsed two shadowy riders bent over their horses. He could not be absolutely positive, but one of them was the dark-clad figure of Cal, the counterfeiter. The other rider could have been Finn Tucker. He dug hard after them and was raising his Colt to get off a shot when he realized it was still empty.

He looked down at his empty weapon. For just a moment he had the foolish feeling it had betrayed him. Then, shaking his head ruefully at such nonsense, he turned and started back to the sad group behind the cabin, reloading both his Colt and the derringer as he went.

While Matt Swenson went back to the ridge for their horses and for a slicker he could wrap Randy in, Longarm and Ty inspected the field of battle. They found two men severely wounded; the rest—six in all—were dead. Longarm had accounted for three of them: the two he had shot with his colt and the one he had taken down with his derringer. The man Longarm had pistol-whipped was still in the bedroom, groaning. Inspecting him closely, Longarm noted that the man would live, but would not be able to eat steak for a while. He took the outlaw's weapon, dragged him up onto the cot, and left him.

Ty was administering to one of the severely wounded outlaws who had fallen in front of the cabin. He stood up as Longarm approached. "This one's bleeding like a stuck pig. I think it was Matt got him as he came running out of the cabin."

"Do what you can for him. I want to check out this building over here."

Ty nodded and went back to the dying man. As Longarm passed him, he recognized him as one of the cardplayers. The fellow had, Longarm recalled, been a very serious player, one who preferred to stay at the table while the rest roamed about. He should have stayed at the table, Longarm mused bleakly as he crossed the compound and entered the long building.

146

At once he was assailed by the strong smell of good ink and well-oiled machinery. He found a lamp, lit it, and hung it on a wall hook. The place was filled with the paraphernalia an experienced engraver would need. There were cans of ink stacked along the far wall, cartons of paper—and, gleaming in the corner, the printing press. It seemed far too elaborate a press for the needs to which it must have been put. Moving close to it, Longarm found the counterfeiter's workbench. It was littered with ink-soiled cloth, etching tools, and wooden blocks.

But no plates. Longarm swore and began to search thoroughly, a conviction growing within him that he was not going to find what he was looking for; that Calvin Fredricks had taken those plates with him when he galloped out of here. He kept at the search, nevertheless, until he had exhausted every possible hiding place, then straightened up with a sigh and started for the door.

It opened and a tall, hulking figure blocked the doorway. The light from the lantern fell full upon his face and Longarm saw that it was Frank Tarnell. The man's entire right side was encased in a shell of coagulated blood. Bits of grass and particles of leaves were embedded in the blood. The man must have dragged himself a long distance to get to this building.

"I saw you come in here," the man rasped, lifting the sixgun he held in his hand. "I want you, Long. I want you bad."

The gun wavered in the big man's fist. Longarm saw the awesome pain etched in the man's face and mirrored in his eyes.

"Put it down, Frank," Longarm said quietly. "You're a dead man already."

"I know that, you son of a bitch. But I want to take you with me."

"Go ahead, then."

Tarnell's face stiffened, and a kind of shadow fell over it. He gasped and slumped sideways, then slipped all the way to the floor. Longarm saw Ty, his gleaming weapon

147

out, standing in the night outside.

"I didn't want to hit the poor son of a bitch," Ty said softly. "But I saw what he was up to and came running."

Longarm nodded and inspected the fallen oak of a man. Ty had creased his skull with the blow from his sixgun, and the man was unconscious. It did not look to Longarm as though he would ever regain consciousness. He had been wounded twice, both rounds entering his chest. How he had managed to crawl from where he had fallen to this building was a miracle of will—and a tribute to his desire to kill Longarm.

Longarm straightened and stepped over Frank Tarnell's body. That accounted for all of them. He knew now who he had seen riding from the hollow: the counterfeiter and Finn Tucker.

And if Longarm's hunch about Cal's identity was correct, he had a pretty good idea where those two men were heading.

As Matt Swenson pulled up, he turned his bleak face to Longarm.

"I'll leave you here," he told them. "There's a spot back of the farm I think was Randy's favorite. I'll build her a coffin and bury her there."

"I'll be back to pay my respects," Longarm told the man. "And to pick you up."

"I expect that."

With a curt nod to Longarm and Ty, Matt pulled his horse around, its sad burden resting across his pommel, and rode off in the direction of his farm. Longarm watched him go for a while, then turned to Ty.

"I'm going to Pine Tree City, Ty. I thank you for your help. But I think I can take care of this business now."

"Without my help."

"It ain't that I don't need it. But you've already done enough. And I thank you."

"That scratch of mine doesn't hurt worth a damn. And I'd like a personal introduction to that woman you said

148

might be able to sew up my shirt. Mind if I stick with you a while longer?"

Longarm smiled at the man. "Suit yourself, Ty."

"It suits me fine."

It had been dawn when they parted from Swenson; it was the middle of the afternoon when they rode finally into Pine Tree City. They dismounted inside the livery, where Hank regarded Longarm and Ty curiously. "You two gents back here lookin' for more trouble, are you?"

Longarm said, "That's about the size of it, Hank."

"Well, it rode in here last night, during the wee hours of the mornin'."

"And where's it staying?"

"At the hotel."

"Much obliged."

As Longarm and Ty left the livery stable, Ty said, "I'll check out the Cowboy's Palace. I got a hunch that's where I'll find Finn."

"And as I told you, more than likely the man I'm looking for is holed up somewhere he doesn't have to show that ruined face of his."

"In the hotel."

"That's right. Ironic, ain't it?"

"It is if he's the man you think he is—and if that girl in there really is his daughter." He shook his head. "You watch yourself. I'll be in to see you as soon as I check out the saloon."

Longarm nodded and continued on to the hotel as Ty crossed the intersection and disappeared through the saloon's batwings. Beverly was startled, then overjoyed to see Longarm standing in her doorway. She hugged him with the strength of a mother bear, then pulled him quickly into the suite and closed the door.

"You look all tuckered out, Longarm, but you're in one piece, and that's a comfort for these sore eyes," she cried happily.

"Now that you mention it," agreed Longarm with a

149

smile, "I am a mite saddle-worn, at that. I think this poor ass of mine would love to feel that big soft sofa of yours under it."

"Now, you go right over there and sit down. You hungry? I can have the girl rustle something up—coffee, anyway."

"Coffee would be fine, Beverly."

As Longarm eased himself into the sofa, he felt the weariness fall over him like a shroud. It wasn't just body-weariness resulting from so many hours in the saddle without sleep; it was a profound weariness of the soul that blanketed him. He closed his eyes momentarily and saw once again Randy's body lying in the moonlight, her life ebbing away through the hole made by a bullet meant for him.

Over and over during this long ride, he had tried to understand what it had been about him that had caused that tough, plucky girl to decide his life was worth hers. Also, in his mind's eye, Longarm kept seeing that bedroom of hers before it had been torn apart by the mad dogs that had come for her. He sighed wearily and realized that he would never again be able to see a bedspread and curtains of that shade of lavender without thinking also of Randy's pale face shining in the moonlight, and Matt Swenson, sobbing silently, as he bent over her. . . .

He was being shaken softly, gently. He awoke with a rush of panic, reaching for his Colt, then relaxed as he saw Beverly's face smiling down at him. Behind her stood Ty, looking weary, but relieved to see him. Longarm sat up swiftly, apologetically.

"When I came back with the coffee, Longarm," Beverly explained, "you were asleep. So I just hauled those big feet of yours up onto the sofa and threw a blanket over you. You don't mind, do you?"

Longarm ran his long fingers through his hair and smiled sheepishly up at them. "I suspicion I was a deal more tuck-

150

ered out than I realized, at that. Where's that coffee, Beverly? I think I could use a cup—maybe two."

As she hustled out of the room, Ty sat down on the chair across from him. "While you were getting your beauty sleep, I dealt myself into a card game at the Cowboy's Palace."

"What did you find out?"

"Those two rode in here all right, but they haven't showed a whisker since."

"They're in this hotel, then."

Ty nodded. "Of course, at the time they got in, Beverly was not on the desk. Most likely she doesn't have any idea who her new guests are."

"But we can find the room easy enough."

Ty smiled. "I have already checked the register. A Mr. Smith and a Mr. Tucker. Room fourteen, on the second floor." He glanced ironically up at the ceiling. "Directly over our heads, as a matter of fact."

As Beverly hustled into the room with a pot of coffee and three cups on a tray, Longarm glanced out a window and saw that night had already fallen over Pine Tree City. He must have slept for some time. There was a good chance that this was why Finn Tucker and Cal had not yet shown themselves. They had probably been just as exhausted as he had been upon reaching this place.

Sipping the hot coffee, Longarm leaned back and watched Beverly. She seemed so pleased that Longarm was back safe and sound that he hated to destroy her composure with the bizarre news that there was a possibility that one of the guests in her hotel was her long-sought-for father, the man who had helped drive her sister mad.

"How's Anne?" Longarm asked her.

The contentment on Beverly's face vanished. "The same, Longarm. Yesterday, she appeared to be coming out of it. I thought I caught her actually looking at me as I cleaned up the bedroom. But I must have been wrong. When I tried to speak to her, it was hopeless." She sighed. "I know I

151

shouldn't use that word, but I am afraid that is how I am coming to feel."

"You're right, Beverly," Longarm chided her gently. "You shouldn't use that word."

Ty cleared his throat. Longarm glanced at him.

"You want me to wait outside, Longarm?" the man asked.

Longarm thought for a moment, considering Ty's question. Ty was thinking of Beverly's feelings. Like Longarm, he knew what the next step would most logically be, and that what Longarm had to tell Beverly would not be pleasant.

"No, Ty," he said. "I won't be long." As he said this, he looked at Beverly.

"What is it, Longarm?" She had caught the tension in the air.

"You have two new guests. They arrived last night."

"Yes, I know. I didn't see them, but I know one of them. Finn Tucker."

"It's the other one I'm thinking about," he told her carefully.

He saw her round face go suddenly pale. She had been standing by the other end of the sofa. Quickly she sat down on the end cushion, her dimpled hand moving to her face, her eyes growing slowly wider.

"Calvin . . . ?" she asked, her voice hushed. "He's here?"

"I don't know. I mean, like I told you before, his name is Cal and he *is* an engraver. He's the one been making the bogus bills with those stolen plates. I suspicion he still has them and that as soon as they can, him and Finn Tucker are going to hide out somewhere and start printing their own fortune. That's what I can be pretty sure of, Beverly. Whether or not this man is your father, that I don't know."

"But . . . you're pretty sure."

"I'd have to find out from him what his last name is, Beverly. He'd have to tell me without him knowing why I want the information. Or I'd have to find that out some other way."

152

"Or I could talk to him," she said, her voice stronger now, her face determined.

"Yes."

She took a deep breath, then downed her coffee in one gulp. "I need something stronger in this," she said, getting swiftly to her feet.

Longarm glanced at Ty. "She'll do," he said. "She's a tough one."

"She'll have to be," remarked Ty.

About fifteen minutes later, Beverly left the suite, her face grim but determined, her nerves fortified with a stiff shot of whiskey, neat. She returned to the suite in less than five minutes. Closing the door behind her, she leaned back against it, her face pale.

"Well?" Longarm asked softly.

She bobbed her head quickly, stiffly, obviously trying to hold back the tears. "It's him, all right," she said. "I'd recognize that voice anywhere. I asked them if they wanted their supper sent up. Finn Tucker answered and said he did, but . . . my father . . . he said not to send it up. They were arguing some as I started back down the hall."

"Leave the rest up to us," Longarm told her.

She nodded, still holding back her emotions. He did not know precisely what she was feeling. It was concern for her father, undoubtedly—but there must have been a good portion of rage as well. Beverly loved her sister. She could not but hate anyone who had turned her sister into the silent vegetable she had now become, no matter how unwittingly that person may have contributed to her condition. Longarm thought he could see those two conflicting emotions warring on her countenance.

He got up and went over to her. She bowed her head gratefully and Longarm took her in his arms. "I'm sorry, Beverly," he said as she began to sob quietly, like a small child. "Maybe I could have taken the man without your needing to know what he did. But if he goes with us peaceful, he'll have to serve time in a federal prison. And he *is* your father. You'll want to know where he is. He'll need your help."

"I understand," she said weakly. "You did right, Longarm." She looked up into his face then, tears streaming down the heavily rouged and powdered face. "You are a kind man. You don't mean to hurt anyone on purpose. I understand that."

Longarm led Beverly over to the sofa. As she sat down, he told her, "We're going up there now, Beverly, as long as they're still in the room. It'll be easier than taking them outside. You stay down here with Anne and keep your head down. There might just be some lead flying before this is over with."

She nodded.

Longarm turned to Ty. "Let's go."

Leaving Beverly's suite, they headed for the stairs. As they passed in front of the registration desk, Longarm told the oldtimer at the desk that it might be a good idea if he went for a drink. The old man stared at Longarm for a minute, confused, then abruptly began to move. Ty was ahead of Longarm on the stairs, but Longarm caught up with him as they approached room fourteen. They were as silent as shadows as they paused just outside the door. Longarm leaned his ear against the door's panel, his gun drawn.

The sound of the two men inside arguing came to him clearly. It was not a wild argument, just a surly, disagreeable interchange that appeared to be getting nowhere, more like a quarrel between a husband and wife than between two outlaws. The room was obviously getting on Finn Tucker's nerves, while Cal was insisting on their both staying where they were until it got later. Finn wanted a drink, evidently—and maybe some companionship a little more comely than this man with the ruined visage.

Once Longarm had some idea of the placement of the two men in the room, he moved back from the door and pointed to his right, indicating that Ty should be ready to

154

take the one in that direction. Ty nodded. Longarm stepped back, lifted his foot, and kicked the door viciously, just above the latch.

The doorjamb splintered as the ancient door swung open. Longarm was through it even before it struck the wall, with Ty on his heels, his sixgun trained on Finn Tucker, who—fully clothed, boots and all—was reclining on the bed, his back against the brass headboard, a tattered mail-order catalogue in his hands. Cal was standing by the window, his dark suit immaculate, his black bandanna fitted about his lower face. Longarm wondered in that instant if Cal remembered when, thrusting his face close to Longarm's, he had yanked down the bandanna to give Longarm a closer look.

His gun leveled on the man's midsection, Longarm barked, "Don't make any sudden moves, Calvin. This don't have to cost you nothin' but time."

The man's black, cold eyes regarded Longarm balefully. "You mean time in the federal prison."

"That's right. For counterfeiting."

"We can deal! I'll let you have the plates! They're genuine! Think how you could use them!"

Longarm pretended interest. He let his eyes light up some. "You have them with you?" he asked, lowering the muzzle of his Colt just a little.

"Of course!" the man cried.

"Show me."

"It's a deal?"

"I said show me."

"Don't listen to the son of a bitch, Cal!" cried Finn Tucker from the bed. "He won't go over. He's too goddamn straight!"

Cal's nervous glance flicked from Finn to Longarm. If Longarm could have seen the man's lower face, Cal's tongue would most likely be licking his lips nervously. "Once you have them, you'll see what riches they can bring you," the man cried. As he spoke, he hurried behind the

155

bed and bent to pick up a carpetbag that had been placed under it. He rested the bag on the bed and swiftly opened it.

But his hand did not come up with the plates. He had a huge Walker-Colt in his fist instead. At the same moment, Finn Tucker swept the kerosene lamp off the nightstand beside the bed and flung the lamp at Longarm. As the revolver in Cal's hand thundered, Longarm ducked to avoid the lamp. The slug from Cal's gun shattered the mirror over the dresser just as the lamp struck the wall and exploded.

As flames swept up the wall, Finn Tucker charged the startled Ty, overran him, and bolted out the door. With a scream of rage, his carpetbag clutched in his hand, Cal followed out after him. Longarm was thinking of Beverly as he tracked the man across the bed—and did not pull the trigger. This man was, after all, her father.

And then both men were gone.

"Hellfire!" Longarm cried, enraged at his own incompetence, and raced out of the room after them.

Two shots greeted him, and Longarm ducked back into the blazing room. Ty, getting to his feet, looked wide-eyed at Longarm. "They're out there?"

"That's right," said Longarm bitterly. "They ain't going nowhere. They're out there and waiting on us. You all right?"

"That son of a bitch managed to hit me on my wounded shoulder as he went by. I would have taken him, Longarm, if I'd been able to hold the gun in my right hand."

"It's getting hot in here. We've got to think of a way out of this room besides the hallway."

Shielding himself from the flames that were now licking along the ceiling, Longarm darted to the window. Less than five feet below it, he saw a small back porch roof. It would be an easy jump if the roof would hold. He lifted the window. At once the flames took on an even greater vitality. It seemed that with that one action, he had turned the room into an inferno.

156

"Hurry up!" he cried to Ty. "This way!"

Longarm saw Ty start toward him. The bed was in his way. He stepped up onto it, shielding his head and shoulders with his arms. But the footing on the mattress was unsteady and he stumbled, sprawling forward onto the bed. The flames, by that time, had drawn a fearsome curtain between Longarm and Ty. Only dimly now could he see Ty. He tried to reach back to the bed and grab the man's reaching hand, but the heat was too intense. He felt his eyebrows singeing and pulled back.

He heard Ty scream then, and saw the man writhing on the bed as the bedsheets appeared to erupt in flames. The man began to roll frantically. Longarm glimpsed his face, twisted in pain, as he scrambled madly to his feet and, blazing from head to foot, leaped from the bed and charged out through the doorway.

Through the roaring of the flames, Longarm heard the two shots. With a groan, he turned back to the window and lifted it still higher. The roar behind him increased. He holstered his Colt, then jumped. He struck the slanting roof, felt it shift under his weight, then dropped as lightly as he could to the ground.

He was not alone in the back alley. A crowd had gathered to watch the fire. But as Longarm got to his feet, they fled back into the shadows. From around the corner of the blazing building, Cal appeared, his carpetbag in one hand, his big Walker-Colt in the other, pointed at Longarm's chest.

"We got that son of a bitch, Marshal!" the man cried. "He took two slugs in his chest. Too bad. We did him a favor. We should have let him burn."

Finn Tucker appeared beside Cal, his gun out also. "Too bad you didn't stay up there, Marshal," Finn said, grinning, the orange glare of the flames giving his face a satanic cast. "You'dve gone to hell a mite sooner."

"But he's going there now," Cal said, raising the big gun carefully and sighting along its enormous barrel.

But the next shot did not come from Cal's Walker-Colt.

157

It came from the corner of the building behind him. Cal jerked, then staggered forward and dropped to the alley floor on all fours. For a moment he tried to get up and raise his gun to fire on Longarm. Then he gave it up as a bad job and collapsed facedown. Longarm had drawn his own weapon the moment the shot had been fired. Now, as he crabbed sideways, snapping off a shot at the fleeing Tucker, he saw Beverly, an enormous rifle at her shoulder, stepping out from behind the corner of the hotel and heading for the wounded man twisting slowly on the ground—her father, the man she had just shot.

158

# Chapter 14

Longarm reached the wounded man's side just as Beverly did. Dropping beside him, he glanced up at Beverly and asked if Anne was safe.

"I took her to the girls at the Palace," she told him, through the tears coursing down her cheeks.

Longarm turned his attention back to Beverly's father. The man was still very much alive; as Longarm reached under him for the carpetbag containing the plates, Cal snatched at it and looked up at Longarm. The bandanna had slipped from his face.

"Damn you! These are mine! I'm not dead yet!"

Then he saw Beverly standing over him, the rifle still in her hand. "Beverly," he cried. "Was it you shot me? But all this time it was I who had been protecting you from these men. That was my deal with Tarnell!"

"Was it?" Longarm inquired.

"Yes! I did not want Beverly to see me like this. I knew she had come out here to find me, but how could I admit to her what I was—and how could I bear to have her recoil every time she looked upon me? I have been damned, sir!"

"By yourself," Beverly told him, her voice bitter, the tears still streaming down her cheeks. "Damned utterly."

A crowd of men had gathered, their faces livid in the glow from the flames that were now devouring the hotel

159

beside them. The night air was filled with sparks. Soon, Longarm realized, the entire town would be aflame if someone did not organize a bucket brigade to wet down some roofs and siding. But no one crowding upon the wounded man seemed to care about that.

They knew about the plates, Longarm realized. Swiftly, he pulled the carpetbag out from under Cal Fredricks. Then he unholstered his Colt and held it lightly in his hand as he glanced about him at the enclosing ring of faces.

"I'll shoot the first one of you that makes any sudden grab for this satchel," he told them.

A voice from the rear cried, "We know what's in that bag, Marshal. And we don't think you're gonna put them plates to good use."

Raucous laughter greeted that remark.

"Good. Then you know what I'll do to prevent you—any of you—from taking these plates from me. Now get back. All of you!"

Reluctantly, the crowd of men began to fade back. A few faces glanced up at the fierce flames now reaching into the night sky. It was perhaps beginning to dawn on them that they might lose their town—their refuge. A few broke from the ranks of encircling men and began running from the back alley, crying out for the others to follow them and help form a bucket brigade. This was enough to galvanize, finally, most of the others. Soon, only a few men were still crouching in the firelit darkness, watching Longarm as he got to his feet and stood beside Beverly over the fallen man.

"Beverly," Cal called weakly. "Help me up."

"No," she said.

"But why? I am your father! Do as I say, woman!"

Beverly looked at Longarm then. She was torn. Though she had just shot her father down to save Longarm's life—this man writhing in pain on the ground before her was still her father.

"Go see to Anne," Longarm told her. "She will need you soon if these flames spread. I'll tend to this man."

160

Beverly just nodded, dropped the rifle to the ground, and hurried off through the hellish night, her face bowed in her hands as she went.

Cal Fredricks pushed himself to a sitting position. His face was a frightening sight, made even more so by the pain etched on it and the dancing flames now towering over both of them giving his countenance an appropriately infernal cast. "Damn you, sir! You have the upper hand now. Will you not at least help me to my feet? Must I be abandoned here by you, to be consumed by these flames?"

Longarm moved closer, then went down on one knee to look the man fully in the face. "That might be right and just, mister. There's a friend of mine up there in that burning hallway that you and Finn cut down. So I'm not going to be easy with you. I'm going to tell you who you are."

The man recoiled from the bitter loathing he detected in Longarm's voice. "Save your lectures, Marshal. This is not a revival meeting. You cannot save me."

"That's right. I can't. You are damned, and that's a fact."

The man struggled to get up. He reached out to Longarm. Longarm stood up and stepped back. "Listen to me, Fredricks. You say you protected your daughter from the men in this town. It was a deal you made with Tarnell and his gang."

"Yes. They were to give her no trouble. Or I would cease to work with them. It was the only payment I required for my skills."

"You had two daughters, Fredricks."

"I know that."

"Where is the other one?"

"In Connecticut. She's married."

"Is she?"

The man frowned. Through the pain of his wound he was beginning to realize that Longarm indeed had something to tell him. A shadow of fear fell over his ravaged face. "What is all this, Marshall? If your aim is to torment

161

me to death, I'd appreciate a bullet instead." He reached his hand out. "Help me up, I say."

Longarm pulled the man to his feet. It was plain then that his wound, though painful, was hardly fatal. Longarm saw a bloody smear running down his left side. The man wobbled slightly when Longarm released his hand.

"Now, what is this about my youngest daughter?" Fredricks demanded. "What are you trying to tell me?"

"She's no longer married, and she's no longer in Connecticut."

The man frowned. "How so?"

"She came out here to be with her sister."

"With Beverly?"

"And to find you."

"You say she's here—in this town?"

"Yes. And she found you. You and your friends, the Tarnell brothers."

The man was confused. "I . . . I don't understand what you are trying to say, Marshal. What . . . what do you mean, she found me? I do not recall meeting my youngest daughter." He paused then, as an insane thought passed momentarily through his mind, only to be dismissed instantly as too horrible to be accepted.

"Oh, yes, Fredricks, you met your youngest daughter. I saw you with her. You and Finn Tucker. If you'll remember, it was I who took her from you—and brought her back here to her sister."

The man groaned, then collapsed onto his knees.

"Yes, Fredricks," Longarm told him. "That girl you drove mad—that girl you took over and over again—was your daughter, Anne. She went looking for you. And she found you. She did not know who you were, I reckon, because of the scars on your face—but maybe, after a while, something in your voice might have reminded her . . ."

"Stop!" the man cried, clapping his hands over his ears.

He lurched to his feet and spun about in a complete circle like a madman. His eyes were wild, his mouth twisted into a silent scream. He was remembering, Longarm realized—

162

remembering every moment he had spent with Anne in that tiny bedroom. He was seeing again the way she had been used, over and over again, by the others.

And perhaps, also, he was able to understand finally why so many of the girl's mannerisms had reminded him of someone he once knew. . . .

He went mad before Longarm's eyes, flung himself about again, and, lurching horribly, plunged past Longarm toward the burning building. A keening cry of despair shattered the night, to die only when the man had disappeared through the flaming back doorway into the inferno.

The next morning, Longarm rode out of a smoking ruin that had once been Pine Tree City. All but one of the saloons had been gutted, and the remaining saloon had lost its front porch. Hank's livery had been saved. But not much else. Beverly was still in the place with Anne, but she was making plans to purchase a carriage from Hank and had promised Longarm that she would ride to Northfield as soon as she could, that she would put the horror she had witnessed in Pine Tree City behind her and take Anne back to Connecticut. He hoped she meant it.

Longarm had much unfinished business still before him. Not only was he anxious to track down Finn Tucker, but he had a score to settle with Matt Swenson as well. Matt had told Longarm that he was expecting him.

And Longarm did not intend to disappoint him.

Longarm came upon Randy's fresh grave before he reached the farmhouse.

He pulled up and gazed down at it for a few moments, trying to remember the girl's laughter, hoping to see in his mind's eye one final, pleasing image he could carry with him that would wipe out the sadness of that other, final image of her, lying under the stars, her life draining away.

It came to him then. He saw her lashing out defiantly with her hand, slapping Finn Tucker—outraged and indomitable, more than a match for any man in that room. He

163

nodded to himself. Yes, that was how he would remember her.

He turned the black and put it into an easy lope toward the farmhouse below. As he rode up, Matt Swenson, cradling a rifle in his arms, stepped out of the kitchen door and picked his way carefully down the sagging steps.

Longarm rode into the yard and reined in the black; then he chucked his hat back off his forehead and folded his arms. "That's a nice spot, where you buried Randy."

The man pulled up a few feet from Longarm's mount, the rifle still resting casually in the crook of his right arm. "I planted a sapling beside the grave. It'll be a fine elm someday. Randy would like that."

"I am sure of it."

"You've come to take me in, have you?"

"I have."

"I could kill you. By the time you reached for that Colt of yours, I could blast you out of your saddle."

"You could at that."

"But you don't think I will."

"Matt, you're going to have to serve more time. But after you do, you'll be able to come back here and watch that tree grow. That's a certainty. If you try to raise that rifle, on the other hand, that's not so certain, after all. I didn't get this old by not knowing how to draw my iron fast enough—even faster then the Last Great Western Bandit."

A slow, reluctant smile creased Matt's rugged face. "Yeah," he said. "That's what Randy used to call me, sure enough." He lowered the rifle still further. "Light and rest a spell. I got coffee on. The ride into Northfield's a long one."

Longarm noticed it at about the same time Matt did—the glint of sunlight on a gun barrel in a grove of trees ahead of them—a grove through which they would soon be riding. Longarm pulled up and regarded the trail ahead of him thoughtfully.

164

"You got good eyes for a lawman," Matt drawled, pulling up also. "Looks like you got a welcoming committee waiting for you in them trees."

"Looks like it."

"You got anything else besides me that's valuable?"

"In this carpetbag," Longarm replied, patting the satchel riding behind his cantle, tied securely to his bedroll. "The federal plates Cal was using."

"Why don't you let the Last Great Western Bandit handle this, Longarm?"

"What have you got in mind?"

"Deception."

"I'm listening."

"Let me take your Colt and hold it on you as we ride. When we get close enough to them trees so the jasper in there with that rifle can see I got the drop on you, I'll call out to him and offer to deal."

Longarm regarded Matt for a moment, considering the proposal. It wasn't that he didn't trust the man; it was just that he realized what a temptation he was dangling before him if he went along with this admittedly clever ruse.

"All right," he said, slipping Matt his Colt.

Pleased at the trust this action of Longarm's represented, Matt said, "You won't regret it. That's a promise."

"We'd better start up, then, before whoever it is gets suspicious."

They were almost to the trees when a voice from among them called out, "What you got there, Matt?"

Longarm recognized the voice immediately; it was Finn Tucker.

"I got me a lawman, Finn," Matt called back. "Got the drop on the son of a bitch with his own iron." He laughed then, and it suddenly occurred to Longarm that Matt Swenson might be in cahoots with Tucker—that this whole ride up to this point could have been a ruse to lull him into letting down his guard.

Before he could do anything to counter what he suddenly felt might be a trap, Finn Tucker, aboard a big roan, spurred

165

out of the trees, his rifle trained on Longarm, a pleased smile on his face.

"Hell, Matt," the man exclaimed, "I thought I was going to have to kill the bastard to get them plates he must be carrying." He laughed aloud, then, as he rode closer. "'Course, maybe I still might have to kill him—so no federal officer will know what happened to the plates."

"That might be a good idea at that," Matt said agreeably.

"And I want you to know, Matt, that I'm cutting you in if you want. How does that sound to you?"

"Sounds just fine," Matt said, and smiled amiably as he raised Longarm's Colt and fired two quick rounds into Finn Tucker's face.

Finn was flung backward off his horse and crunched to the ground, landing headfirst. His mount reared in fright, wheeled about, and galloped frantically back toward the trees. Matt handed Longarm his Colt, butt-first.

"Couldn't help myself, Longarm," the man said, staring bitterly down at the sprawled figure. "He was one of them animals that took my daughter. Guess he didn't think I minded that—the poor stupid son of a bitch." The man shuddered then, as if a terrible chill had run up his spine. "Let's go," he said. "The man's stench turns my stomach."

Without a word, Longarm holstered his gun, clapped his spurs to the black's flanks, and rode on past the dead man. His horse shied a bit, forcing Longarm to skirt rather widely the dead outlaw. He glanced at Matt as the man spurred his mount to keep up with Longarm's black.

"I owe you an apology, Matt," Longarm told the man. "I had a few moments back there when I regretted handing you my gun."

"Knew you would. But you got plenty of sand and didn't let on. I appreciate that. I had an idea that was Finn Tucker waiting for us. Saw him riding on ahead before you got to my place. I wanted him. Wanted him bad."

"You could still have kept my gun. You had the drop on me."

166

"Nope. You'd be a fool and try to take it from me. I know the kind of lawman you are. Met a few Pinkertons in my day just as tenacious. Yessir." He looked at Longarm then and grinned. "You're a powerfully lucky man, Longarm."

"How so?"

"You think I tried to kill you back there when I was raiding them freight wagons."

"Of course."

"Mister, when I take my time like that and aim good and proper, I don't miss."

Longarm frowned and pulled up his horse. The animal swung its head in irritation. "What are you trying to tell me, Matt?"

"That I didn't aim to kill you. I aimed to miss, to give you a mean headache, and that's all."

"But why?"

"Randy. She told me about you. Said she liked you and said you was the one ventilated some of Tarnell's men after they mistreated her. I figured I owed you, Longarm. But them gents with me wanted your scalp, especially that poor gent you wounded. So I made it look good to satisfy them."

"You made it look good, all right. Have you noticed the gash in the side of my skull?"

"You got plenty of hair. It'll grow over—like an old brand."

Longarm started his horse forward again. "That's what everyone's been telling me."

"It will. I can hardly see it now."

Longarm frowned. "Then I owe you. Twice. For what you did—and of course for what Randy did for me, as well."

"Don't you let it worry you none. I know you got a job to do."

"Yes, I have. And I'll do it. I have to, Matt. I'm the law."

"You don't have to explain anything to me. I just told

167

you that so you'd understand why I couldn't ever kill you. It'd be a damn fool thing for me to kill a man whose life I saved." His face grew somber then. "And a man Randy gave her life for."

"Matt, we're going to need your testimony to put away Beazley and Wiggins. If you'll do that, I'll speak to the judge for you. It may help some."

"Well, I'd sure appreciate it, but it ain't nothin' you have to do."

Longarm nodded. Matt was right, of course. There was nothing Longarm *had* to do—except bring in his man. It was as simple as that.

# Chapter 15

By the time Longarm and Matt Swenson clattered across the iron bridge that spanned Cannon River, the entire male population of Northfield, it seemed, was aware of their approach. Work had apparently halted at news of their coming, and now, as Longarm rode across Mill Square on his way to the sheriff's office, he saw the boardwalks crowded with gawking townsmen and shopkeepers.

A few men called out cheery greetings to Matt, and others saluted Longarm solemnly. It was apparent to Longarm that not a few of those watching the two of them ride past were surprised to see Longarm alive—and startled to see Matt Swenson his prisoner.

Dismounting in front of the sheriff's office, Longarm was greeted by a breathless hardware clerk, still resplendent in his denim apron and green-visored cap.

"Marshal!" he cried. "I just saw the sheriff riding out of town!"

"Which way did he go?"

"North."

"Much obliged."

Longarm led Matt into the sheriff's office and looked around for the keys to the lockup in back. He found them on what had been deputy Tod Wiggins' desk, and escorted Matt to a cell. As he closed the cell door on Matt, Longarm

169

felt a twinge. Matt must have seen Longarm's reluctance in his face because the old bandit spoke up gently as Longarm turned the key in the door's lock.

"Now don't you go feelin' sorry for me, Longarm. I been in prisons before. It's the price an outlaw has to pay. He expects it—if he has any sense, that is."

Longarm nodded, turned, and left the cell block. He knew that what Matt said made sense; every outlaw should understand that at one time or another his luck was going to run out. What bothered Longarm about Matt, though, was how a man who could think as clearly and reasonably as that would let himself become an outlaw in the first place.

The town marshal was exactly where Longarm had expected him to be, lubricating his throat in the Daisy Miller Saloon. The moment Longarm's tall figure pushed its way through the batwings, the place went silent. Behind him in the street, Longarm could hear the running footsteps, the pleased, excited shouts that brought still more spectators. As Longarm started to walk toward the town marshal, the door to Daisy's office opened and Daisy hurried out to greet him.

He touched the brim of his hat as she pulled up before him. She was flushed with the pleasure of seeing him again. If the place had not been filled with greedy-eyed men, she would have flung her arms about his neck.

"You're back, Longarm!"

"And with all my bolts and hinges in place. It's good to see you again, Daisy."

"I have some Maryland rye. Would you come in for a drink?"

Longarm shook his head. With some reluctance, he said, "I have to sober up this town marshal holding up your bar first, Daisy. Then I've got a couple of polecats that need collecting." He grinned down at her. "You know the ones I mean."

"Yes," she said, "I do. One of them's been in here,

170

bragging you'd never come back alive from Wolf Hollow."

"Bill Wiggins?"

"Yes."

"Figured he'd be in here crowing some, soon's he got back." Then, in a voice loud enough for every man in the saloon to hear, Longarm said, "He left his brother dead in the Badlands. Lit out and never gave a backward look."

This news was a sensation. Longarm heard the whisper of it sweep the saloon and then reach the crowd outside the saloon.

"You keep that Maryland rye ready, Daisy," Longarm told her. "I won't be long."

Then Longarm reached out and pulled the town marshal from the bar. The man almost collapsed without the bar to support him. He grabbed at his hat as Longarm swung him around and then booted him toward the batwings, sending him windmilling through the doors. When Longarm reached the street, he saw the man, supported by several grinning townsmen, waiting for him.

Longarm plucked him from the townsmen and sent him stumbling ahead of him down the street. "You're the new sheriff in this here town, Marshal," Longarm told him. "I want you to stay in that office and keep a watch on my prisoners. You leave the place to tickle your tonsils any more today and I'll ream your ass with that useless sixgun at your side."

The crowd keeping up with Longarm appreciated that, and there seemed to be a visible stiffening of the town marshal's spine as he began to walk ahead of Longarm. He was a slightly built, sandy-haired incompetent with washed-out eyes and a feeble cough; but for now, anyway, he was going to have to do.

Longarm had become a traveling show. As he reached the Wiggins Emporium in search of Bill Wiggins, the growing crowd that had followed him from the saloon to the sheriff's office pulled up to watch. To Longarm, the crowd felt like

171

a waiting animal at his back as he entered the general store and approached a clerk, who appeared to be trying to disappear behind a root beer barrel.

"Where's your boss?" Longarm demanded.

The clerk quaked. Snatching at the pencil he kept stuck behind his ear, he pointed to a door behind the main counter. "He's in that room, Marshall!" the man cried, his voice quavering. "But he's armed. He says he won't come out of there alive!"

"That just might be," Longarm said laconically, as he left the clerk and approached the door.

With the barrel of his Colt, he rapped smartly on the door. "Come on out, Bill. Matt Swenson's in a cell waiting for you to join him."

"Get away! I won't be locked up, I tell you! I'd rather die first."

"Suit yourself," Longarm called through the door.

"I'll kill myself first," Bill wailed.

Shifting his Colt to his left hand, Longarm snatched a small keg of nails up off the counter behind him and hurled it with considerable force at the flimsy door. The keg hit just above the doorknob. The door flew open, revealing a cringing Bill Wiggins crouching down behind his desk, the barrel of a sixgun in his mouth, his eyes wide.

"Go ahead, Wiggins," said Longarm, striding into the small office. "Pull the trigger. Save me from doing it."

"No!" the man cried, yanking the gun from his mouth. "Don't shoot!"

With a single quick swipe, Longarm knocked the revolver from Wiggins' hand with the barrel of his Colt. As the sixgun clattered to the floor amid the explosion of nails that now covered it, Wiggins shrank back, his arm shielding his face.

"Don't hit me!" the man cried, his voice almost as high as a woman's.

"I'd like to, but I won't—as long as you come quietly and stop all this foolishness. There's a crowd out there

172

waiting. If I was you, I'd pull myself together some. It won't look good. Some of those men out there you'll be needing as character witnesses when you come to trial. See if you can't act like a man, at least until I get you into that cell."

"Your tone is insufferable," snarled Wiggins. He straightened up behind his desk, apparently convinced that Longarm was not going to shoot him.

"That's better," Longarm said.

He reached over then, grabbed the man by the shoulder, and pulled him out from behind the desk. A moment later, as the two emerged from the general store, a cheer went up from the waiting crowd.

Well, Longarm mused, if there were character witnesses in the crowd, they sure as hell weren't going to be giving testimony that would be of much help to Bill Wiggins.

Longarm was glad to leave the crowd behind when he rode out of town an hour later. Heading north aboard the black, he did not have to travel far before he picked up the sheriff's trail.

Reaching a sandy wash beside a narrow stream, Longarm dismounted and inspected the tracks of a laboring horse that was obviously being pushed to its limit, the gait so uneven that Longarm wondered how the animal could remain on its feet under Beazley's enormous bulk. Mounting up again, Longarm guided his horse across the shallow stream and followed the tracks toward a hump of tree-shrouded hills in the distance. Beyond those hills—well beyond, Longarm realized—was the Canadian border, but the tall lawman had no confidence at all in the porcine sheriff's chances of reaching it.

Two hours later, Longarm pulled up and peered carefully through a grove of willows. He had just caught the shine of a roan's rump. He sat his horse patiently and watched. The roan moved out from behind the trees. It was the sheriff's roan, all right; it was still saddled as it grazed

173

peacefully along the banks of a wide stream.

So where was sheriff Beazley?

Longarm nudged his horse forward until the roan's head bobbed up, ears flicking. Abruptly, it turned and loped off, heading downstream. Longarm spurred his black after the roan. In less than a mile, it led Longarm to the forlorn figure of the sheriff, sitting on a tuft of grass along the bank of the stream.

The man didn't even bother to turn around as he rode up.

"Is that the softest spot you could find?" Longarm inquired.

Beazley turned to look up at Longarm. "I'm all blisters, you son of a bitch. I need medical assistance."

"That so?"

"Yes, damn you!"

Longarm dismounted. With a gentle voice and persistence, he managed to grab the roan's reins and lead it back to where the sheriff still sat on his cool tuft of grass.

"I'm taking you back, Sheriff."

"And just how do you propose to do that? I cannot ride in this condition."

"Sure you can. It won't be easy and it might sting some, but you can ride." Longarm was smiling when the sheriff flung himself around to stare at him in horror.

"I tell you I can't ride! I refuse! And where's your warrant?"

"Right here," Longarm said, patting his holstered Colt.

"By God! I believe you are serious."

"You'll ride my black. That roan's been through enough. I figure the black can take it better than the roan can. Let's go."

"Now, see here!"

Longarm was through talking. He walked over to the sheriff and hauled the man to his feet. The big fellow swayed drunkenly. Longarm drew his Colt and poked the muzzle up under the sheriff's nose.

174

"You keep on arguing, Sheriff, and this here pistol's liable to go off. I wouldn't have to haul you all the way back to Northfield then, and this poor animal of mine wouldn't have to suffer like that poor roan. Is my meaning clear?"

Longarm thought the sheriff was going to cry so he grabbed the sheriff's vest and flung him angrily at his black. Blubbering like a schoolboy, the man reached out for the black's stirrups to prevent himself from falling. Longarm strode up behind him and kicked him smartly in the rump. With a sudden and remarkable alacrity, the obese sheriff flung himself up onto the horse.

It was only when he lowered his posterior onto the hard leather of the seat that he began to perspire. "I hope you rot in hell for this!" he cried down to Longarm.

Longarm smiled up at the man. "The way I figure it, the devil himself ought to give me a medal for this afternoon's work. Hang on now."

Longarm mounted the roan, took up the black's reins, and rode back up the stream at a nice, steady trot, pulling the black after him.

He pretended not to hear the sheriff's screams.

Slipping into his frock coat, Longarm left Daisy's bedroom and strode through her sitting room to her office. Daisy, a petulant frown on her face, followed him, tying the sash to her long black velvet nightgown.

"A nightcap, Longarm?" she asked.

"Yes, Daisy. Thank you." Longarm sat down in the upholstered chair, beside which he had placed his hat—and took a deep breath. Daisy certainly knew how to say "welcome back," he told himself contentedly, as he watched her hurry from the room to get the Maryland rye.

When she returned with the bottle of rye and his glass, her petulant frown had hardened noticeably. "Really, Longarm," she said, placing the tray on the table beside his chair, "my feelings are hurt. We have the whole night. Why ever

175

in the world did you take a room at the hotel? You know you could have stayed here with me. Did the prospect so terrify you?"

He laughed gently as he poured his drink. "Not at all, Daisy. But I've already given you my reasons for taking that room. I'm thinking of your safety."

"Those federal plates?"

He nodded and sipped his drink. "Finn Tucker was not the only one who knew I took those plates from Cal Fredricks. They ain't counterfeit plates, don't forget, but genuine plates. For the right man, those plates could mean a fortune. That's a powerful prod, Daisy. If I have to fight off any desperate men after those plates, I'd rather do it in my hotel room than here. You ain't as likely to get struck down by any stray bullets. Besides," he said, smiling, "I'm usually in a position to defend myself when I'm alone in a hotel room."

"Yes," she said, smiling. "I guess I can understand that."

"There's one thing about all this that still has me puzzled, Daisy."

"What's that?"

"I'm having trouble placing the bank cashier, Paul Welland. I still don't know what he was doing near Randy's place and why Tarnell's gang murdered him."

She smiled, like a little girl who has kept a secret long enough. "Perhaps I can tell you."

"If you know, I purely wish you would, Daisy."

"I think it was Welland who alerted the government to the fact that those bills were being passed here. He wanted an investigation of Tarnell's gang."

"He didn't seem very enthusiastic when I questioned him."

She smiled. "He had changed his mind by then. He knew he had made a mistake and was afraid for his life."

Longarm frowned. "So he rode to warn Tarnell."

"Yes."

"But they already knew what he had done and killed him the moment he showed himself; is that it?"

176

"Something like that. Of course, I can't be sure."

"How did you learn all this?"

"You forget my business, Longarm. This saloon is the most popular meeting place for the men in this community—and for those outside, as well."

"Tarnell was in this saloon when I arrived in Northfield?"

"One of his men. Tip Wilcox."

Longarm nodded. "I met the man. We didn't get along."

"Mike heard most of it. It is really surprising how loudly men talk after a few whiskeys, no matter how delicate the business."

"I can imagine."

She smiled proudly at him. "There! Have I settled that matter for you?"

"Not entirely, Daisy."

"Oh?"

"What would make a man want to double-cross a gang as powerful as the Tarnell gang? I am figuring, of course, that he was in cahoots with them—a perfect front, in fact, if they wanted to pass their fake bills."

"Yes, I believe he was working with them."

"So why would he double-cross them?"

Her face flushed slightly, her hand reaching up and stroking her long, lovely neck absently. "He . . . he was in love with me, Longarm."

"And you put him up to it?"

"It was not like that at all," she said hastily. "But when he confided to me what he was doing, I told him I could not consider taking a man seriously if that man was a criminal."

"I see."

"Do you, Longarm? Can you imagine what marriage to a man on the run must be like? I have seen such women. It is not pleasant. When I told him that . . . he did as I told you. He had some fool notion that if he was responsible for the capture of that gang, I would reconsider."

"He was wrong."

"Of course he was wrong. You saw what happened to

177

him. I can't imagine what made him think he could get away with such a scheme against that gang."

"I can imagine, Daisy."

"You can?"

"He was in love with you."

"Well, I was *not* in love with him. He was a fool."

"So Mike heard Wilcox planning to bushwhack me before I left Northfield."

"Yes. Tip left before you did. I imagine Welland ran into the gang on his way to warn Tarnell."

Longarm finished his drink and stood up. "Thank you, Daisy," he said, "for a lovely evening—and of course for the Maryland rye."

"You sure you won't stay the night? Your precious plates will be safe here. I promise you."

He smiled, then kissed her lightly on the cheek. "Don't forget. I have to get up sometime tomorrow and start a long train ride to Denver. You would leave me too light to walk, woman."

"Yes, I would," she said devilishly.

She walked him to the door. As she pulled it open, he turned to her.

"Would it be too late for me to visit the saloon's kitchen? I'd like to take something over to my room with me."

"Go ahead in there. If they're cleaning up still, you just tell them I told you it was all right."

He kissed her lightly. "Much obliged, Daisy, and goodnight."

As Longarm pulled himself out of the barber's chair the next morning, he found that the barber would not accept payment.

"Are you sure?" Longarm asked, startled by this evidence of his fame.

"Marshal Long, you have already paid me—and I will remember that payment for the rest of my life—and so will most of this town."

"I don't understand."

178

"I do," said the other barber, at the next chair, leaving his customer reclined almost parallel to the floor, his face swathed in steaming cloths. "It was the sight of that sheriff, screaming bloody murder, tied to your horse—as you brought him in. They ought to pass laws against men that fat riding horses."

Longarm's barber grinned happily at the thought. "He sure won't be riding again soon—not with an ass full of blisters, he won't."

Longarm thanked his barber and left the shop, pausing on the sidewalk to appreciate the bright morning. He had visited the telegraph office earlier to get off a telegram to Vail, and had purchased a ticket for later in the day. He was vaguely troubled, however. He knew that he had accomplished what he had been sent out here to do; he had the plates in his possession. And yet he could not shake the feeling that he was not finished—that he hadn't really got to the end of that twisted ball of twine he had encountered when first he arrived in Northfield. What Daisy had told him about Welland the night before had been of some help, but still . . . there was a nagging uncertainty that would not give him rest.

He was starting to cross the street to his hotel when he saw Daisy's bartender hurrying along the boardwalk toward him, a growing crowd on his heels. Longarm turned to wait for Mike.

"Mr. Long!" the man cried. "He's got Daisy!"

"Hold it. Now just hold it right there. *Who's* got Daisy?"

"Bill Wiggins. He broke out. That damn town marshal got drunk and let Bill and the rest of them out. Bill promised the marshal he'd give him enough money to buy a saloon of his own. What he gave him was a mean crack on the head."

"What do you mean, Bill Wiggins has got Daisy?"

"He's got her in her office. He says if anyone comes near him to take him back to prison, he'll kill her."

"And he will, too!" cried a little man behind Mike.

"What does he want?" Longarm asked shrewdly. He

179

knew suddenly that Bill had a plan that went far beyond holding Daisy Miller hostage in her own saloon.

"He wants you to let him get on the next train out of here. And he'll kill Daisy if you try to keep him from leaving!"

"What else does he want?"

"Them federal plates."

"Then I guess there's nothing for it but to give 'em to him. Can you tell me—is Daisy all right? Has Wiggins hurt her?"

The little fellow spoke up again. "He ain't hurt Daisy, not yet, he ain't. But he might, Marshal. He's a wild man. I never seen the like."

Longarm turned to Mike. "Come with me to the hotel. I'll get the plates."

Longarm left Mike downstairs in the lobby while he hurried up the stairs to his room. Once inside, he locked the door behind him and lifted the carpetbag onto the bed. Reaching into it, he took out and unwrapped the inkstained paper that enclosed the plates. Then he reached under his mattress and pulled out the two flatirons he had taken from Daisy's kitchen the night before.

As he had done as a precaution before going to bed, he replaced the federal plates with the flatirons, wrapped them in the paper that had enclosed the plates, and placed them back in the carpetbag. After secreting the federal plates under the mattress at the head of the bed, Longarm hurried from the room with the carpetbag.

Downstairs in the lobby, he handed the carpetbag to Mike. The lobby was crowded with citizens eager to hear every word that passed between them.

"Now listen, Mike. You tell Bill Wiggins that if he harms Daisy, I'll come after him—and it don't matter what hole he crawls into, I'll find him. Can you remember that, Mike?"

"Sure, Marshal, I'll remember."

"You tell him. Just what I told you."

180

As Mike started to go, the crowd following him, Longcharm said, "One more thing. When is that next train pulling into the station, Mike?"

"In about two hours," Mike replied.

Longarm nodded, watched Mike and the onlookers bull their way out of the lobby, then waited a moment longer before leaving the hotel and heading for the livery stable.

Longarm scrunched down in his seat as the train pulled into the Northfield station, then pulled his hat down farther over his face. To anyone passing him in the aisle, he looked like one more passenger trying to sleep. Though his face was almost completely hidden by the brim of his hat, Longarm was able to see the entire station platform—and the excited crowd that packed it.

He had no difficulty picking out Bill Wiggins and his hostage.

Wiggins was clutching the carpetbag in one hand, a revolver in the other. A sullen, angry-looking Daisy was close beside him, and as the train ground to a halt, she turned to look at it with bleak eyes.

Wiggins shouted something to the crowd, and a few of those standing closest to him backed hastily away. Then, waving his gun menacingly, Wiggins pushed Daisy toward the train. She glanced back over her shoulder, as if she could not believe the townspeople would allow this madman to take her with him.

A moment later both Daisy and Wiggins vanished from Longarm's sight as they climbed aboard the train. Longarm was about to turn away from the window when he saw Matt Swenson dart from the back of the crowd and hurry to the rear of the train. In a moment, he too had disappeared from sight.

The door at the front end of the coach swung open, and a grim-faced Wiggins entered, pushing Daisy roughly ahead of him. Longarm ducked his head as Wiggins glanced quickly up and down the coach. He did not look up again until the train began to move. He saw that Wiggins and

181

Daisy were sitting four seats in front of him, on the side of the train away from the platform. Daisy was sitting next to the window, and the carpetbag had been stashed in the carriage rack over their seat.

As the train picked up speed, Wiggins and Daisy appeared to relax. In a moment, the train passed over the Cannon River. Daisy laughed suddenly, a delicious, wicked laugh that filled the coach. A few passengers, obviously warmed by the sound of Daisy's laughter, turned to look at her and Wiggins.

Longarm got up, turned around, walked to the rear of the coach, and opened the door. Stepping through the doorway, he saw that the train, traveling slowly as it clicked across a tangle of switches was slowing still further as it approached a turn. Longarm swung down onto the steps, hung for a moment by the handrail, then dropped lightly to the ground. He landed running, then pulled up and climbed the embankment.

As he did so, he glanced at the rear coach. Matt Swenson was looking out at him in astonishment. Longarm smiled at the man and waved. For a moment, Matt was too startled to respond; then he smiled broadly and waved back.

By the time Longarm had hoofed his way back to Division Street, the townspeople had left the station. Still excited by the sensational events of this morning, however, knots of people were standing about everywhere, talking animatedly among themselves.

As one of the townsmen saw Longarm walk past, he called out, "Too bad, Marshal! Can't win 'em all!"

"True enough," Longarm replied, and kept going.

When he entered the sheriff's office a moment later, Longarm was not surprised to find Sheriff Beazley sitting glumly inside his cell—even though the door was apparently unlocked. As Longarm paused before the bars and looked down at him, the big man glared up at him and shook his head bitterly.

182

"No sense in my making a run for it," he told Longarm. "I can't hardly move—thanks to you."

"Right sorry about that," Longarm said.

"You sound it."

Longarm left the office and started down the street for the Daisy Miller Saloon. He was almost there when he heard his name called.

He spun about to see Beverly Fredricks hurrying across the street toward him. Longarm went to meet her.

"What are you doing in Northfield, Beverly?" he asked.

"What am I doing here?" she asked. laughing. "I am at the moment busy listening to the wild goings-on of this place. And I've heard much about you—and that poor Daisy Miller. You've lost the plates, I understand."

"Bill Wiggins has them."

"That's what I heard."

"You can't win 'em all, Beverly."

She shook her head.

"How is Anne?"

"Longarm, we drove into Northfield in a buggy I purchased from Hank, and do you know what? During the drive, Anne began to sing softly to herself. I asked her what she was singing, without even expecting an answer—and she told me. She said, 'Don't you remember, Beverly? We used to sing it together after church in the living room.'"

"That sounds promising. You mean she is coming out of it?"

"Not yet, Longarm. But I think she's better. She didn't say much after she stopped singing that song, and right now she's as quiet as ever. One of the girls who used to work for me in Pine Tree City is with me. She's taking care of Anne now. We're going back to Connecticut."

"I think that's a good idea. You didn't lose everything in that fire?"

"A successful madam always keeps something in a stocking, Longarm."

He laughed. "Good luck, Beverly. If Anne ever comes

183.

out of it, give her a kiss for me."

"I will, Longarm."

He watched her return across the street, feeling pleased all of a sudden; then he turned around and continued on to the Daisy Miller. The place was boiling with people, even though it was no later than eleven o'clock in the morning. At Longarm's entrance, an aisle was made for him so that he could reach the bar. It seemed that his apparent failure to prevent Daisy Miller's abduction had diminished his popularity not one whit—a measure of how much the people of Northfield detested Sheriff Beazley, Longarm had no doubt.

As Mike paused before him to take his order, Longarm said, "Maryland rye."

Mike laughed and reached under the bar for the bottle. As he poured, Longarm said casually, "How much did Daisy sell you the place for, Mike?"

The man almost dropped the bottle.

"Finish pouring, Mike. Then maybe you and I can go into Daisy's office for a chat. That suit you?"

The man swallowed. "Sure, Marshal."

A moment later, a very nervous barkeep closed the door securely behind him and joined Longarm, who was sitting in his favorite chair. Mike sat on the edge of the sofa and asked nervously, "What makes you think Daisy sold me this place, Marshal?"

"She wouldn't leave it without selling it—if she owned it, that is."

Mike moistened dry lips. "You're right, Marshal. She didn't own it. I did. I bought it from her a long time ago."

"Gambling debts?"

He nodded. "But they weren't hers. A high-toned gambler came by a year ago. Daisy fell for him pretty hard. He was sure lucky in love, all right—because he wasn't so lucky at cards. Daisy bailed him out each time, though—until the poor son of a bitch got himself shot by one of Tarnell's boys."

184

"Cheating?"

"That's what they said."

"So you stayed behind the bar as the silent partner—and no one knew Daisy no longer owned the saloon."

Mike nodded wearily. He had no idea what Longarm would do with this information, and he was frightened.

"You mean no one knew but Bill Wiggins."

Again Mike nodded, this time rather sheepishly.

Longarm leaned back in the upholstered chair. He had all his answers now. It was Daisy who had made Welland betray Tarnell's secret. She had wanted those plates. But Welland had lost his nerve and gotten himself killed. So, as a last resort, she had obtained them through the aid of the ever-willing Bill Wiggins.

Daisy had probably planned to leave the train at the next stop, where no doubt she had already arranged to have horses and supplies waiting. They would very likely ride a good long way before the time came for them to unwrap that ink-smeared package and gloat.

He wished for a moment that he could be on hand when Daisy discovered what she had given up for those two flatirons. And what she had gained, as well. Bill Wiggins was not going to make an ideal companion in the months, and possibly years, ahead. Which was why Longarm had left them in that train coach together.

Longarm shuddered. Sometimes he was too cruel.

He got to his feet. "Thank you, Mike. I wish you a lot of luck with this saloon. Are you going to change the name?"

"Not on your life. Why, it's famous now."

"So it is."

As Longarm left the saloon and headed across the street to the hotel, he realized that his own train would be pulling in pretty soon, and he still had to pack up the real plates and ride back to the next town to retrieve the black he had left there when he boarded the train for Northfield.

185

He decided suddenly that he would send Vail another telegram. He could leave the next day. Meanwhile, he might look up Beverly, see if she needed anything. She might be a big woman physically, but that didn't bother Longarm; she had a heart that was more than enough to satisfy him.

**SPECIAL PREVIEW**

Here are the opening scenes
from

*LONGARM AND THE GOLDEN LADY*

thirty-second in the bold
*LONGARM* series from Jove

# Chapter 1

The rising sun winced painfully at the brim of the contorted horizon like some hungover eye winking up red and reluctant from the bottom of a whiskey bottle.

Longarm slumped in the government-issue saddle cinched upon an exhausted agency-leased Morgan horse. A tall man, lean and muscular, he let the patient animal trudge at its own gait up the first rise of the timber-fringed slope into Denver, finishing the ten-mile trek from Eldorado Valley at a walk.

It had been a long, sleepless night. He and the horse were bone-tired, but at least they were alive. They had lived through one more night following longlooper tracks, but the man wrapped in a soogan and sagging across the Morgan's back behind him was dead.

You kill one, Longarm thought, and Texas Bill Wirt recruits three more owlhoots to take his place. They come up like fleas in a buffalo robe, wild-eyed and hotheaded, anxious to make a gun rep and quick bucks with a lawless band of sidewinders.

189

He tilted his head, raising the flat-brimmed Stetson, snuff-brown and worn dead center, angled slightly forward, cavalry-style. Pink-flushing sunlight touched at his sharp-hewn face, seared and cured to saddle-leather brown by raw sun and cutting winds and ornamented by a drooping long-horn moustache that augmented the hard ferocity of his appearance. His tired eyes shone a gunmetal blue, his close-cropped hair, showing under his hatbrim, was the color of aged tobacco leaf. He wore skintight brown tweed pants, as snug as his skin, and low-heeled cavalry stovepipe boots, more suited for running than riding. His frock coat was buttoned tightly against the Colorado night chill, and though he'd been eternal hours in the saddle, his string tie was still knotted at the throat of his gray flannel shirt.

He turned easily in the saddle, catlike, and shifted his eyes warily along the narrow street as the first houses hove into sight. He wasn't expecting trouble, but he was prepared for it—out of nowhere, which is where it usually came from. There was nothing in the atmosphere to alarm him; nothing more than his instincts. He was on guard.

He saw no one along the long street, and for this he muttered a silent prayer of thanks. At 5:00 A.M., it was early, even for the good people of Denver, to whom lazing abed past dawn was one of the Seven Deadly Sins. Thank God he had the streets to himself. All he wanted was to get his outlaw's carcass to the sheriff's office as quickly and unobtrusively as possible—and without any accidents.

Longarm kept his coattail pushed back just clear of his cross-drawn-holstered Colt .44-40. As tired as he was, as near home as he was, he didn't want any surprises.

He glanced about in the silent morning. He couldn't explain what troubled him. He'd feel fine as hen's teeth, though dog-tired, if only there weren't this unexplained premonition of wrong, working at the nape of his neck.

He sighed heavily. Accidents. Accidents were mistakes you made when you relaxed and let down your guard. Accidents had a way of happening sudden. And accidents

190

could be fatal. The fellow yoked across the horse's rump behind him was the victim of such an accident. The outlaw had accidentally drawn on Longarm when he was down, mistakenly thinking him disarmed as well as prostrate.

"We all make mistakes," Longarm allowed across his wide shoulder. "The fewer we make, the longer we last."

Longarm listened to the patient plodding of his horse's hooves on the hardpacked red clay street. Poplars, elms, and cottonwoods lined the quiet yards. He smelled the first promise of breakfast fires, saw the first pale lamps wink to life at curtained windows closed tightly against the threatening night vapors.

He mused on the youth he had slain in the line of duty and who the boy might be. Law enforcement got brutal sometimes, but it was necessary if good people were to live safely among the human wolves. A kid like this ... Who was he? Where'd he come from? What made him prey on law-abiding people? What made him join a band of rattlers like Texas Bill Wirt's gang of thieves? What made him draw his gun when he had only to go quietly—and live?

Longarm glanced over his shoulder. He'd thought Texas Bill Wirt's killer legion might ride after him last night, but then he'd realized that this kid, dead, meant nothing to the longloopers anymore. Wirt's men had abandoned the kid to slow Longarm down. Now the boy was dead and nobody cared.

Longarm shivered slightly in the morning chill. It was a waste, a hellish waste, that's what it was.

He glanced east, lifting his head enough so the crimson sun turned his dark moustache red.

His horse carried him and his dead captive into town at a plodding walk, knees and hocks bending tiredly, withers quivering. The sun-splotched streets lay empty at this hour. The long trek was almost over. A body delivered, a report made, oats and a rubdown for his horse, and ten hours in the sack for him. He'd earned it.

His first warning of peril was the sudden thud of boots

191

at a run on the red ground behind him. Behind him? Certainly, where else? Trouble never came easy upon you, only fast.

"Longarm!"

The raging baritone voice, pitched low in the chest to give it power and authority, blasted silence out of the morning.

Longarm's nerves twisted, something congealed in the pit of his stomach. He felt the horse shudder under him at the raucous yell, spooked. Longarm used wrists and knees in an automatic gesture, moving the Morgan into a turn in the middle of the street. As his animal sidled, he drew his gun and crabbed from his saddle, landing on his parted feet, legs set, with the horse as his shield.

Longarm stared, angered but not startled. The kid yelling his name looked like any other saddle tramp under twenty, coyote-lean, hungry-eyed, unwashed, frayed and tousled, with an outsized weapon in a tied-down holster low on his hips. The looks of the kid told everything one needed to know about him. Another young hellion on the prod, looking to make a name for himself as the man who killed Custis Long. Only Longarm wasn't ready to go yet.

Longarm stepped from behind his horse, letting the reins trail. He further demonstrated his contempt by slapping his Colt angrily back into its holster. "What you want, boy?"

"Don't call me boy, you son of a bitch."

"Get back under your rock and I won't call you at all."

They faced each other on the silent street. "Your name Longarm?"

"My friends call me Longarm. You can call me Long. *Mister* Long."

The boy's laughter fluted oddly. It sounded empty-bellied, tense. The kid probably hadn't eaten breakfast, maybe no supper last night. His precarious circumstances made him as edgily dangerous as his motives—whatever in hell they were. "Smart old man, ain't you, Long?"

"Smart enough to stay alive to *get* this old, boy." Long-

192

arm shrugged his wide shoulders. "Now if that's all you got to say, I'm in a hurry."

"You stand where you are, rooster." The boy's voice cracked, brittle with rage. "I'll say when you can go."

"I'm gettin' fed up with this, boy."

"I told you, Long. Don't call me boy. You'll know I'm a man before I'm through with you."

Longarm peered through the dazzling dawn light at the scrawny youth, seeing another rootless kid consumed by a terrible pride and driven by some restless compulsion to prove himself to a world that couldn't care less. He shrugged again, turned, and reached down to take up the dangling reins.

"You move and I'll shoot you in the back, you fat son of a bitch," the boy yelled.

Longarm grinned sourly and shook his head. He supposed the underfed kid saw anyone who had eaten even recently as fat. He felt a flaring of pity for the boy, but his pity was marinated in weary irritation—the very worst kind of savage impatience.

"I ask you one more time, boy. What you want with me?" Longarm jerked his head toward the corpse tied across his horse. "You know this hombre? That what's eatin' you?"

"No. I don't know him. I don't care about him. It's *you* I'm after, Long."

Longarm exhaled heavily, unobtrusively slapping his coattail back from his high-belted holster. "You mind saying why?"

The boy grinned wolfishly, seeing that Longarm had bared his weapon; this was the kind of respect the boy liked to see; it was too infrequently accorded him. He had no way of knowing Longarm was a cautious lawman. He would have done as much for a sidewinder. The boy shifted his weight on his scuffed boots. "You know Cotton Younger?"

"Cole Younger? Jesse James's cousin?"

"You heard me, old man. Cotton Younger. You know him?"

193

In the space of a breath, Longarm sorted through the outlaws stored in the files of his mind. Cotton Younger. A brother of Cole Younger and a cousin or something of the James boys. One of the Cole Younger–Jesse James gang who had terrorized the frontier from Minnesota to Missouri. Cotton had escaped the law. He had disappeared completely. He was a hard man to hide because he was named for his sandy eyebrows, faded blue eyes, and pale yellow hair. Besides which, he was almost seven feet tall; he stood out in any crowd. There was nothing Cotton could do about his height, but he had dyed his hair a fierce black with coal tar and had turned up in that disguise in a Wyoming Territory settlement called Crooked Lance. He'd hired on as a rider for the Rocking H Ranch and soon was bossing the outfit. He had fallen in love with a local belle and could have lived out his life respectable and respected, but he got greedy and ended up a corpse roped across his saddle, like this cadaver from Eldorado Valley.

"I recall the gentleman. Why?"

"Because you shot him down in cold blood, you snivelin' bastard."

"In the line of duty, old son. It was my job. Nothing personal."

The boy shivered like a burro chewing briars. "Well, it's personal with me, killer. You spilt my cousin's blood. I can't live till I avenge his dirty murder."

"You best get your head on straight, partner. It wasn't murder when your cousin Cotton died. Not in anybody's book. Cotton was a federal fugitive—with a price on his head."

"And you kilt him—for the re-ward."

"None of your business, sonny, but marshals can't take rewards or bounties. Like I said, it was strictly business. Now get out of here."

"Oh, no, killer. There ain't no re-ward on you, neither. But I'm killin' you, Long. I'm gunnin' you down as a public service—and to avenge Cousin Cotton Younger."

194

"You even make a move like you're going for that gun, and you're in trouble, kid."

"I'm going for it, Long." The boy flung his arms wide at his sides, standing tensely on the balls of his feet. "You hear me, Long? I'm giving you your chance to slap leather and that there's all I'm givin' you."

Longarm winced. He stared at the ragged boy, standing scrawny and defiant, barely enough of him to throw a shadow. But old enough to kill. A bullet from that boy's gun was as deadly as one from some grown man's hogleg. But he glimpsed the dead youth strapped across his horse's rump. He'd killed his quota of fryers. He wasn't going to kill another one before breakfast. He was damned if he would.

"Get out of here, kid," he said.

"Go for your gun, you lily-livered bastard," the boy said. His sun-faded blue eyes swirled wildly, shadowed with the lust to kill, a madness that named itself righteous hatred. The boy betrayed his move, as if he'd sent a message by Western Union. His arm snaked out and plunged downward toward the low-slung holster.

As the boy's hand tipped the butt of his tied-down gun, Longarm fired.

He had drawn with such dazzling speed that the youth, stunned, hesitated, incredulous. The kid's face turned deathly white as he realized he was about to be killed—and that he'd asked for it, never even suspecting there were men who drew, not by time at all, but by instinct.

Longarm squeezed the trigger on his Colt .44-40 twice so the blasts were almost simultaneous. He seemed to fire instinctively, but he knew better. He held his gun with icy steadiness; even the muscles in his fingers, hand, wrist, and arm were under control of his mind. He aimed his fire as he never had before. He wasn't going to kill this kid, not for all the provocation in this world. Not if there was any other way.

Longarm's first bullet ripped into the youth's holster,

195

into the gun butt, into the boy's hand, gripping the stock, paralyzed. The youth managed to jerk his bleeding hand away, screaming, as the second bullet demolished his sixgun in its holster.

Holding his gun at his side, Longarm walked tiredly toward his would-be killer.

Eyes wide, round, and white-rimmed, the boy watched death stalk inexorably toward him in the misty sunlight.

Involuntarily, the boy began to shake his head. He was numb, helpless, in a trance of agony and fear.

The wounded youth managed to clasp the shattered fingers of his right hand with his left. Blood spurted from the bullet-smashed members with every terrified thud of his heart.

Shaking his head, the boy fell to his knees on the hard-packed street, crying. His shadow seemed to crouch in black agony against him. "Don't kill me, mister. Please. Before God, I beg ya, don't kill me."

"You picked a hell of a time to decide you don't want to die," Longarm said.

"I wanna live, mister. Honest to God, I'm scared to die."

"Sure. All you tramps are. Scared to die. All you ain't scared to do is kill."

Sheriff Marvin Cheeseman poked a dull pencil at the notes he'd made. A lard-bellied man with heavy jowls, he was as near to being a Colorado native as a white man could ever be; both his given name and surname belonged to two of Denver's oldest families. Marvin felt secure in his political position, secure in his own estimation of his self-worth and in his status in the community.

He sat behind his cluttered pinewood desk in a crowded but spacious office in the County Building. His digs were less imposing than those of the U.S. marshal in the new federal complex, but as far as Cheeseman was concerned, the feds had much bigger headaches than he had. Let them keep their swank offices and five-dollar-a-day expense ac-

196

counts; as far as he was concerned, they earned their largesse. He had to keep a tone of satisfaction from his voice. "So you're satisfied Texas Bill Wirt and his men have jumped my county line?"

Longarm shrugged. Chewing an unlit cheroot, he paced the sheriff's office, more aware of his own hunger pangs and his own weariness than of the smug county law official, or of his prisoner, crouched in a chair and nursing his bandaged hand. The doctor had told the kid he wouldn't lose the paw, but he was never going to be a swift-draw. The boy had seemed to melt downward inside himself since they'd left the sawbones. He found little to cheer him in the morning. He was still alive and that was about it.

Longarm said, "Whether Wirt's gang crosses a county line or a state line won't stop us."

Cheeseman managed to conceal his smile. "No. Not you *federales*. But it kind of moves him out of *my* bailiwick, no?"

"That's right. This kid is about all you get out of it. They got away with the money—and until we hunt them down, that's the way it is. I'll leave the kid with you."

"This kid?" Cheeseman frowned, staring at the skinny boy huddled in the hardwood chair. "Didn't understand you to say this kid was one of Texas Bill's riders."

"Not this kid. The corpse. The dead boy. He was left behind as lookout for the Wirt camp. I took him, like I told you. But meantime, Wirt broke camp—or never even slowed down to make one. I think he left the kid just to slow me down until he could lose himself in the Black Lake country. As for crossing the state line, I don't think they will. Not for a while."

Sheriff Cheeseman thrust his bulk forward, his chair squealing dryly. "Why not? What do them desperadoes want around here?"

"I don't know. That's what I wanted to find out. I meant to take the kid alive. He wouldn't have it that way. So I ended up with a corpse. Sometimes you just can't get a lot

197

out of cadavers." Longarm shrugged. "Sometimes not even a name."

The sheriff waved aside the matter of the dead outlaw. "What does Wirt want up here in a civilized place like Denver? Hell, this ain't no hole-in-the-wall country. Not anymore."

"Well, he wants something. Bad enough to risk his hide for it."

"Hell, he can't even show his face on Denver streets. Why, we got Wirt's dodgers up in the post office and in barbershops. We'll let him know we mean business in Denver. That ought to scare him off."

Longarm shook his head. "If the stakes are high enough, nothing will scare Texas Bill off—until he gets what he's after."

"Dammit, Longarm. They kilt two people in that robbery yesterday. Broad daylight. Downtown Denver. Must be easier places closer to home for Texas Bill to rob. Nossir, it's somethin' else he wants up here."

"I agree with you. But I don't know what it is."

"Well, dammit, that's what I want to know. What's Wirt after? What's his gang doing up this far from the Brazos? What's he want in Denver? What's he looking for?"

Longarm smiled tautly around his cheroot. "A profit. I know that much for sure." He sighed. "We'll do what we can, Sheriff. I know Billy Vail won't give up as long as he's got a man ain't too saddle-weary to ride."

"Well, you tell Marshal Vail we can't sit idle and let Texas Bill Wirt and his thugs terrorize the good people of Denver."

"Why don't *you* tell him?" Longarm asked brusquely. It came out harder-sounding than he intended. His personal estimation of Sheriff Cheeseman and his force had nothing to do with it. He had been a long time in the saddle on a futile errand. He'd had to kill a nameless kid who was under twenty—one hell of a lot under. It didn't sit well, and it was unraveling him. Wirt had struck a Denver bank. At

198

least they *thought* it was Texas Bill Wirt—it had all his style and brainless daring—though Texas Bill was reported to be hundreds of miles south in the Texas plains. Wirt was after something bigger than a bank. The people—and a sheriff in an election year—were yelling bloody murder. And he was in the middle. He softened his voice. "We'll do what we can, Sheriff."

"Nossir. That ain't good enough. You feds got to come out from under your own red tape. You don't even know if it *is* Texas Bill Wirt. But whoever it is, it's a murdering gang of desperadoes. They've moved in on us. We want help from you government people. One hell of a lot more'n we're presently gettin'."

Longarm bit down hard on his cigar. "Why don't you write to Washington?" He clamped his hat down, dead center on his crisp brown hair, and strode toward the corridor door.

Sheriff Cheeseman's voice stopped him. "You think I ain't done that? You think I won't—again and again, until I get the support I need? We got big trouble, Long. Bigger than you. Bigger than Vail is willing to admit—"

"And you've got an election coming up—"

"Vail will put more men on this thing, or by God he'll explain to Washington why he don't. I got friends on the Potomac. Don't you people forget it."

"That's between you and Billy Vail, Sheriff." Longarm smiled coldly. "Good morning, sir."

"Just a back-breakin' minute, Longarm. What about this here kid?" The sheriff swiveled his graying head and stared at the shaken youth. "What'd you say your handle was, boy?"

"Jesse Cole, sir." The boy sounded meek. All the starch was sweated down out of him. He cradled his painful hand, practically rocking.

"Yeah." The sheriff looked through the boy, nostrils flared. "What you want me to do with this here Jesse Cole, Long?"

199

Longarm sucked in a deep breath and hesitated, his hand clutching the doorknob. He stared at the boy. It was easy, looking at this scarecrow boy, to forget an arrogant young hellion daring him to draw on that street out there. Hell, this kid was just out of kneepants, just learning to jack off. If he shaved more than twice a week he was wasting lather.

"I'm sorry I tried to draw down on you, Mr. Long. I know you think I'm just sorry because you outdrew me—and could have kilt me. But that ain't it. Not all of it." Jesse Cole tried to smile, looking hound-dog hungry. "I swear, I musta been crazy . . . I never saw nobody draw like you."

Longarm didn't smile. "You're lucky you lived to see it."

"I know that, sir. Like I know now, you was doing your job—when you shot my Cousin Cotton Younger, I mean. I was all mixed up."

"You damn kids," the sheriff said. "You shoot a few bottles off a rock, you outdraw your own shadow a few times, and you git biggety ideas. Going up against an armed man ain't the same as shootin' cans or throwin' down on a cactus."

"Nossir. You're right. And I know I'm almighty lucky to be alive." Jesse Cole lowered his eyes. "I know that. I'm plumb thankful to my maker that Mr. Long is the kinda man he is and all. And I got no right to ask nothing more of either one of you gents. Whatever my medicine is, I'm ready to take it. I've proved I ain't much of a man, but I'm man enough to take my punishment."

Jesse hunched down, turned inward upon himself in remorse and grief, as forlorn as a wet cat.

Longarm swore inwardly. He tossed a dollar on the sheriff's desk. "Hell, there ain't any charges. Feed him breakfast, Sheriff, and let him go. Just so he clears out of Denver."

"I will, Mr. Long. I swear I will." The boy looked up, eyes welling tears. He nodded his head rapidly. "I will. You won't see me no more."

"See that I don't," Longarm said. He walked out, closing the door hard behind him. Damn. Two punk kids in one night. One dead. And the other one? Longarm exhaled heavily. He had no illusions about young Jesse Cole. Jesse was contrite now, scared shitless, ready to beg for mercy. But a kid like that forgot fast. He had to prove himself, prove his own manhood. They had a word for it down on the Mexican border. *Machismo*. A young buck had to prove he had *machismo*. Hell, *machismo* killed more men than heart failure, wives' headaches, and scarlet fever combined.

## EASY COMPANY

Ride the High Plains with the hard-bitten, rough-and-tumble Infantrymen of Outpost Nine as their handsome lieutenant, Matt Kincaid, leads them into battle in the bloody Indian uprisings!

| | | |
|---|---|---|
| —— 05761-4 | EASY COMPANY AND THE SUICIDE BOYS #1<br>John Wesley Howard | $1.95 |
| —— 05804-1 | EASY COMPANY AND THE MEDICINE GUN #2<br>John Wesley Howard | $1.95 |
| —— 05887-4 | EASY COMPANY AND THE GREEN ARROWS #3<br>John Wesley Howard | $1.95 |

And...
Watch for a new *Easy Company* adventure every month from Jove!

*Available at your local bookstore or return this form to:*

**JOVE/BOOK MAILING SERVICE**
P.O. Box 690, Rockville Center, N.Y. 11570

Please enclose 75¢ for postage and handling for one book, 25¢ each add'l. book ($1.50 max.). No cash, CODs or stamps. Total amount enclosed: $_____ in check or money order.

NAME _____

ADDRESS _____

CITY _____ STATE/ZIP _____

*Allow three weeks for delivery.*                          SK-4

★ ★ ★ ★ ★

# JOHN JAKES' KENT FAMILY CHRONICLES

*Stirring tales of epic adventure and soaring romance which tell the story of the proud, passionate men and women who built our nation.*

| | | | |
|---|---|---|---|
| ☐ | 05862-9 | THE BASTARD (#1) | $2.95 |
| ☐ | 05894-7 | THE REBELS (#2) | $2.95 |
| ☐ | 05712-6 | THE SEEKERS (#3) | $2.75 |
| ☐ | 05890-4 | THE FURIES (#4) | $2.95 |
| ☐ | 05891-2 | THE TITANS (#5) | $2.95 |
| ☐ | 05893-9 | THE WARRIORS (#6) | $2.95 |
| ☐ | 05892-0 | THE LAWLESS (#7) | $2.95 |
| ☐ | 05432-1 | THE AMERICANS (#8) | $2.95 |

*Available at your local bookstore or return this form to:*

JOVE PUBLICATIONS, INC.
BOOK MAILING SERVICE
P.O. Box 690, Rockville Centre
New York 11570

Please enclose 75¢ for postage and handling if one book is ordered; 25¢ for each additional book. $1.50 maximum postage and handling charge. No cash, CODs or stamps. Send check or money order.
Total amount enclosed: $_____

NAME_____

ADDRESS_____

CITY_____STATE/ZIP_____ SK-17